D0122675

Dear mouse friends,
Welcome to the world of

Geronimo Stilton

THE RODENT'S GAZETTE
EDITORIAL STAFF

Geronimo Stilton
A learned and brainy mouse; editor of *The Rodent's Gazette*

Thea Stilton
Geronimo's sister and special correspondent at *The Rodent's Gazette*

Trap Stilton
An awful joker; Geronimo's cousin and owner of the store Cheap Junk for Less

Benjamin Stilton
A sweet and loving nine-year-old mouse; Geronimo's favorite nephew

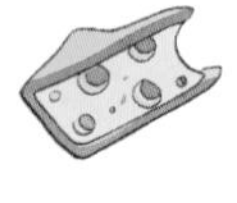

Stilton

THE HUNT FOR THE SECRET PAPYRUS

PLUS a bonus Mini Mystery and cheesy jokes!

Scholastic Inc.

Published by Scholastic Inc., *Publishers since 1920,* 557 Broadway, New York, NY 10012. SCHOLASTIC and associated logos are trademarks and/or registered trademarks of Scholastic Inc.

ISBN 978-0-545-87250-8

Pages i–111
Text by Geronimo Stilton
Original title *Il mistero del Papiro Nero*
Cover by Francesco Castelli (design) and Christian Aliprandi (color)
Illustrations by Alessandro Muscillo (design); Riccardo Sisti (inks); and Daria Cerchi (color)
Graphics by Chiara Cebraro and Francesca Sirianni

Pages 112–193
Text by Geronimo Stilton
Original title *La banda del gatto*
Illustrations by Valeria Brambilla (pencils and ink) and Mirko Babboni (color)
Graphics by Michela Battaglin and Marta Lorini
Fingerprint graphic © NREY/Shutterstock

Special thanks to Shannon Penney and Kathryn Cristaldi
Translated by Lidia Morson Tramontozzi and Andrea Schaffer
Interior design by Becky James

10 9 8 7 6 5 4 3 2 1 16 17 18 19 20

Printed in Malaysia 108
First edition, April 2016

TABLE OF CONTENTS

THE HUNT FOR THE SECRET PAPYRUS

GET YOUR TAIL IN GEAR!

It was dawn on a **frigid** December day. I was snuggled in my comfy bed when the sound of the phone cut my snoring short.

Ring, riing, riiing!

Holey cheese, who could that be?

I opened one EYE, yawned, and lifted the receiver. "Hello? This is Stilton, *Geronimo Stilton*," I mumbled, still half-asleep. "I'm the publisher of *The Rodent's Gazette*, the most famouse newspaper on Mouse Island . . ."

At the other end, a voice **bellowed**, "Oh, really? Well, my name is William Shortpaws! And that paper is only famouse because I founded it! **WAKE UP**, Geronimo — this is your grandfather! You need to get up **immediately**!"

"**G-grandfather? Is that you? It's very e-earl—**" I stammered.

"You're a cheesebrain, Grandson!" he barked. "I just finished reading a copy of today's *Gazette*, and I didn't see any articles in it — not even a sentence or a single photo — about the **BLACK PAPYRUS**!"

Black Papyrus? Moldy mozzarella, I had no idea what he was squeaking about!

Grandfather went on. "When I was running the paper, that kind of thing didn't happen. Do you have even a **morsel** of an idea of what I'm talking about?"

I didn't, but I tried to make something up. "**OHHHH . . . UMMM . . .** the Black Papyrus?" I said slowly. "Papyrus . . . You're talking about **Egypt**, right? Well, it's black because . . . they probably made it out of very dark plants? That makes sense! **Uh . . . right? Gulp!**"

Blushing with embarrassment, I finally admitted, "Cheese niblets, I'm sorry, Grandfather — I don't know what the **BLACK PAPYRUS** is!"

There was a long pause.

"Are you still there?" I asked **timidly**.

Grandfather William suddenly howled, "**I KNEW IT!** What planet do you live on, Geronimo? Get up! **GET YOUR TAIL IN GEAR!** Go to the Egyptian Mouseum in New Mouse City right away! I want you to write an exclusive article about the Black Papyrus. **GOT IT?**"

Before I could answer, he slammed the phone down. Rat-munching rattlesnakes, my grandfather was **ANGRIER** than a caged cat!

That was the first time I'd ever heard anything about the **MYSTERIOUS** Black Papyrus. I had so many questions! There was only one thing to do — I bounded out of bed, and in two shakes of a mouse's tail I was headed to the Egyptian Mouseum.

I wondered: What would I learn?
I wondered: What was the Black Papyrus?
I wondered: Why was it so important?

I wondered . . . I wondered . . .
I wondered . . . I wondered . . .

I LOOKED LIKE A CHEESEBRAIN!

I left in such a **hurry**, I didn't even have time to eat breakfast. Before long, my belly started to rumble like a growling jungle cat. I was hungry! I stopped at the local diner to grab a mozzarella **milkshake** and a small blue cheese **MUFFIN**.

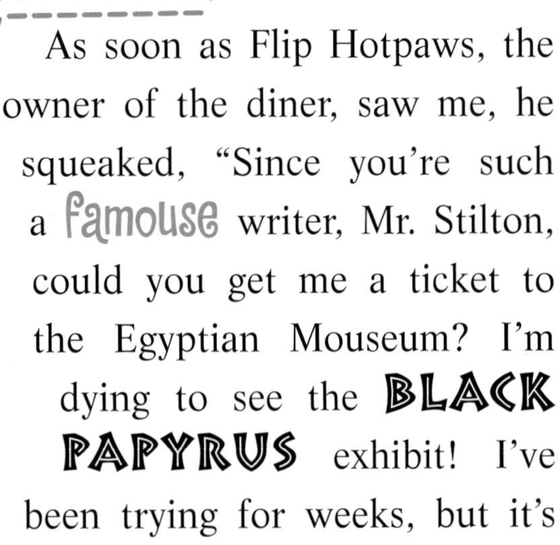

As soon as Flip Hotpaws, the owner of the diner, saw me, he squeaked, "Since you're such a **famouse** writer, Mr. Stilton, could you get me a ticket to the Egyptian Mouseum? I'm dying to see the **BLACK PAPYRUS** exhibit! I've been trying for weeks, but it's impossible to get tickets."

Red with embarrassment, I stammered, "Oh . . . um, what exhibit?"

Flip's whiskers drooped in disappointment. "I thought an intellectual rodent like you would know all about the Black Papyrus!"

Red with embarrassment, I mumbled good-bye and ran to catch the BUS.

I overheard two rodents chatting as I sat down. One said to the other, "You've SEEN the fabumouse Black Papyrus, right?"

Again, my snout turned bright red with embarrassment. Why didn't I know anything about this?

When I arrived at the Egyptian Mouseum,

there was a LOOOONG line outside.

"What are you waiting for?" I asked the rodents in line.

They all turned to stare at me in disbelief.

"You're kidding, right?" one of them squeaked. "This is the line to see the Black Papyrus, the most famouse papyrus in the world. Some of us have been in line since midnight!"

Cheese niblets, now I was red with embarrassment to the tip of my tail!

Suddenly, I spotted my nephew Benjamin and his friend Bugsy Wugsy running TOWARD me.

"Hi, Uncle G!" Benjamin squeaked. "Please tell us the **SECRET** of the Black Papyrus. We're writing an article

for our school newspaper!"

I sighed. How was I the only rodent in New Mouse City who knew nothing about the BLACK PAPYRUS? I had to get into the mouseum — and FAST!

"Follow me!" I said to Benjamin and Bugsy, waving a paw. "We have to find the director of the mouseum, Professor Cyril B. Sandsnout. He'll tell us all about the BLACK PAPYRUS!"

Fortunately, at that moment, the professor appeared in the mouseum entrance.

"I've been waiting for you!" he squeaked. "Your grandfather said you were coming."

To my surprise, my sister, Thea, appeared behind him. "I've been waiting for you, too. Grandfather said that you were writing an article about the Black Papyrus, and he told me to take PICTURES."

THE MYSTERIOUS BLACK PAPYRUS
Finally!
THE MYSTERIOUS BLACK PAPYRUS

A Secret Legend

I'm lucky that Professor Sandsnout is a marvemouse old **friend** of mine. He's an expert on ancient Egypt!

"I'm ready for the interview," he said, leading us to his office. "I'll tell you **everything** I know about the famouse Black Papyrus."

That was **EXACTLY** what I'd hoped!

Professor Sandsnout started filling us in. While I took careful notes, Thea snapped **photos**.

Professor Cyril B. Sandsnout explained why the **BLACK PAPYRUS** was truly one of a kind. We hung on his every squeak.

"This **PAPYRUS** contains the ancient secret of eternal youth!" he said, whiskers

PROFESSOR CYRIL B. SANDSNOUT

First name: **Cyril**

Last name: **Sandsnout**

Nickname: **Desert Rat**

His job: **Director of the Egyptian Mouseum in New Mouse City**

His hobby: **He has an incredible collection of joke books.**

His secret: **He adores playing pranks, especially on his friends!**

THE LEGEND OF THE BLACK PAPYRUS

Pharodent was the youngest pharaoh in Egyptian history. According to legend, he remained young throughout his reign. He wrote the secret of his youth on a special piece of papyrus and hid it.

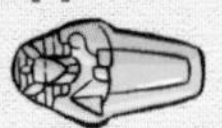

Because this was a truly fabumouse secret, Pharodent recorded it on a very rare type of dark papyrus that grew in only one location. The rare papyrus was harvested by seven rodents, chosen personally by the pharaoh. They dressed in black, painted their snouts black, and gathered the plant only on moonless nights so they wouldn't be spotted.

The secret of Pharodent's youth was written on this black papyrus using the ink of the legendary supersquid that lived in the Nile River. The supersquid was pursued by seven fishermice, chosen by the pharaoh, who fished only on moonless nights. They dressed in black and painted their snouts black, too.

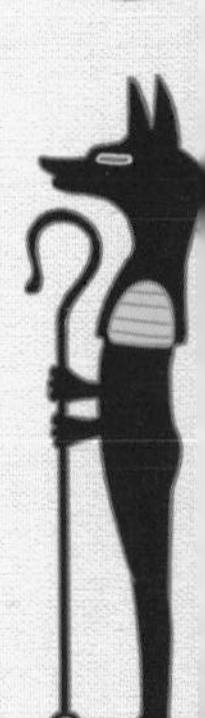

Pharodent lived a marvemousely long life. Before his death, he decreed that the Black Papyrus be buried with him.

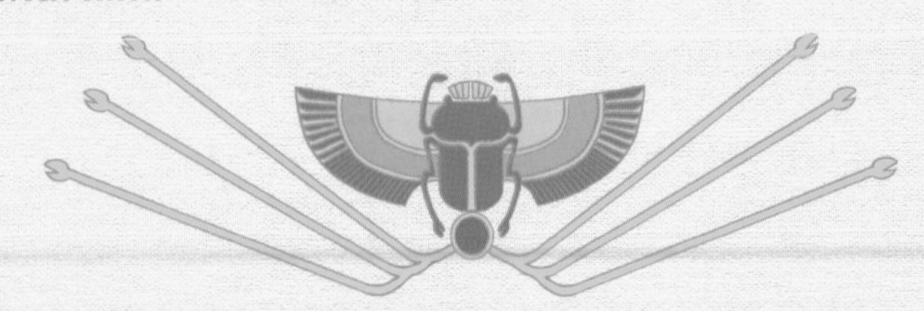

quivering with excitement.

"What's the secret?" my sister asked.

Professor Sandsnout sighed. "Well, that part is still a secret, I'm afraid. We haven't unrolled the papyrus yet to decipher the text. It's a very risky process. The papyrus is so old and fragile, it could easily CRUMBLE!"

Papyrus is a tall, grasslike plant that grows in the Nile River valley. Ancient Egyptians primarily used it to make sheets of writing paper. They soaked the stems in water, pressed them flat, and dried them in the sun to create paper.

He pointed to a dark canvas cloth nearby.

"Under that cloth is an extraordinary machine," he whispered. "It's TOP SECRET!"

Holey cheese, what could it be?

The professor smiled. "I INVENTED the machine myself to unroll the most fragile ancient sheets of papyrus. Tomorrow, I'll use

it to unroll the Black Papyrus, right here in the EGYPTIAN MOUSEUM. It will be televised for the whole world to see. Finally, everyone will know its fabumouse secret!"

He twirled his WHISKERS with satisfaction. "I'm the only one in the world who can unroll the papyrus without the risk of ruining it," he added.

"That's mousetastic, Professor!" exclaimed Bugsy and Benjamin.

Thea walked over to the professor's machine. She was about to lift the cloth and take a photo when he stopped her with a squeak.

"I'm SORRY, Ms. Stilton," Professor Sandsnout said, stepping in front of her. "Even you are **not allowed** to take a photo of it until tomorrow! I can't run the risk of some rat trying to duplicate it before then."

THEA tried her best to change his mind. "But I could get a photo of you, your fabumouse machine, and the Black Papyrus on the **front page** of the newspaper."

She reached over to it again, but the professor gently pushed her paw away.

"Fine," Thea sighed, disappointed. "I guess we'll have to come back tomorrow."

A Suspicious Mouse

Professor Sandsnout walked us to the **DOOR** and waved a paw cheerfully.

"Ancient Egypt was fascinating, and there's still so much to discover! See you all tomorrow, okay?" He looked thoughtful. "Before you leave, you should take a look at the HALL OF HIEROGLYPHICS.

It's FABUMOUSELY impressive!"

Ancient Egyptians wrote by using ideograms (drawings that represent concepts) and phonograms (drawings that represent sounds). Together, these symbols are called hieroglyphics.

We decided to take the professor's advice. There was an entire room in the mouseum dedicated to hieroglyphics (the word for EGYPTIAN WRITING, which was made up of drawings). On display were ancient papyrus fragments, sarcophagi, decorative

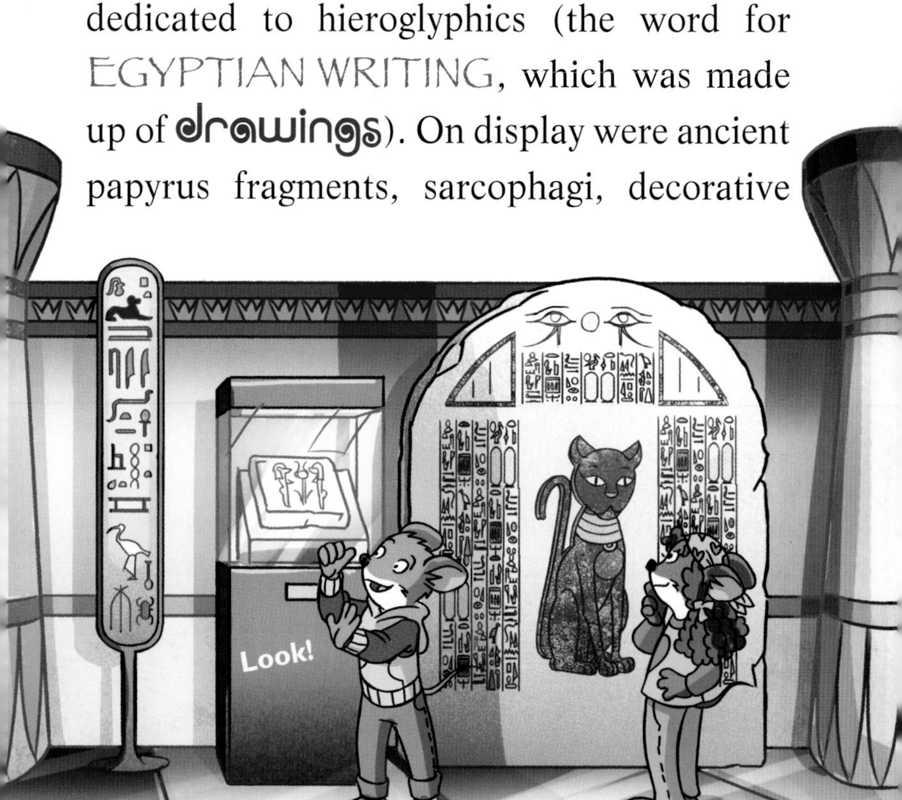

stones, and even a SCULPTURE, all covered with hieroglyphics.

"Look, there's a cat!" Benjamin squeaked.

"A CAT? HEEELP!" I squeaked, my tail twitching in terror.

"Relax, it's not a real cat!" Benjamin said with a giggle. "It's a PAINTING of a cat — here, on this sculpture."

Wobbling whiskers, I had turned as white as a slab of MOZZARELLA! I stepped closer and reached out to touch the stone, but someone stepped in front of my paw . . .

I looked up in surprise and found myself whisker-to-whisker with a **SERIOUS**-looking rodent. His eyes were hidden behind **SERIOUS** dark sunglasses. (He reminded me of someone. But who?)

He had a very **SERIOUS** expression on his snout. (He reminded me of someone. But who?)

He wore a **SERIOUS**-looking black suit. (He reminded me of someone. But who?)

Then the mouse said in a mysterious voice, "If I were you, I wouldn't touch a thing. That's awfully suspicious behavior." He lowered his sunglasses and looked me straight in the eyes. "I'm sorry, I haven't introduced myself. My name is Walt McWhisper."

He lowered his voice and spoke very, very quietly.

"Pssst . . . "

Moldy mozzarella, I couldn't understand a whisker of what he was saying! I LEANED closer.

"Pssst . . . "

I still couldn't **hear**!

Why was Walt McWhisper squeaking so **quietly**?!

I leaned my ear toward him even more, and he whispered, "I'm here on behalf of the M.I.S.S.O., the Mouse Island Secret Service Organization. I'm Agent **00W**!"

A secret agent? Double-twisted rat tails! This could mean only one thing: **TROUBLE AHEAD!**

In the past, I did some work for the **M.I.S.S.O.** — but I'm obviously not allowed to say anything about that assignment. It's **TOP SECRET**!

00W knew that I was also an agent, so he whispered, "**00G**,* listen to me. My cousin, Agent 00K, told me everything."

The dark sunglasses! The serious snout!

* 00G is my secret agent code name!

00W

Name: **Walt McWhisper**
Code name: **00W**
Profession: **Secret agent**
Who he is: **Kornelius von Kickpaw's cousin**
How he became a secret agent: **Since he was a little mouselet, McWhisper has been suspicious of everything and everyone. Kornelius recommended him for a surveillance position at M.I.S.S.O. His job is to be on the lookout for suspicious rodents!**
Notable traits: **He always wears dark sunglasses — and suspects everyone!**

00K

Name: **Kornelius von Kickpaw**
Code name: **00K**
Profession: **Secret agent**
Who he is: **Geronimo Stilton's friend from elementary school**
How he became a secret agent: **No one knows. 00K has worked for the government of Mouse Island's M.I.S.S.O. for a long time, and has led many dangerous missions (including missions in space).**
Notable traits: **He always wears a fancy black suit packed with gadgets — it's ideal for his assignments!**

The black suit! That's who 00W reminded me of — **00K**, otherwise known as my dear friend Kornelius von Kickpaw!

I shook his paw, a little uncertain. Okay, I'll admit it — I felt like a total scaredy-mouse around this rodent!

"Umm, how may I help you?" I asked.

00W lowered his voice even more. "I have a top secret assignment. I'm here to **PROTECT** the Black Papyrus!"

He narrowed his eyes and looked at me suspiciously.

"Why are you here?" he whispered. "Are you trying to uncover the secret of the **BLACK PAPYRUS**?"

I began to whisper, too.

"No, 00 . . . um, I mean, Mr. McWhisper! I'm a journalist, and I'm — "

"Please squeak in a **normal** voice, Mr.

Psst . . . psst . . .

Stilton!" 00W interrupted. "Whispering makes you sound awfully suspicious! Do you have something to hide?"

00W slowly lowered his sunglasses and looked me in the EYES. "Your glasses, for example, look suspicious. Very suspicious. Very, very suspicious!"

For the love of cheese, was he serious? "Without my glasses, I can't even see the tip of my snout!" I explained.

00W held out his paw. “Do you mind?” He pulled a gadget out of his pocket, took off my glasses, and inspected them.

Slimy Swiss cheese! I leaned on a column to steady myself. At least, it looked like a COLUMN to my blurry eyes. But it was actually part of the alarm system! It crashed to the floor and triggered the alarm. The siren wailed.

Suddenly, four mice

dressed in black surrounded me. **Rats!**

OOW immediately started bombarding me with questions. "Mr. Stilton, did you tamper with the alarm? I knew you were a shady rodent! Guards, don't let him GET AWAY!"

I couldn't get away if I wanted to — I was surrounded! Besides . . . I couldn't even see the ends of my whiskers!

"Um . . . could I at least have my glasses back?" I asked timidly, squinting in the direction of OOW.

"Hang on just a minute!" OOW responded,

lowering his voice to a whisper again and leaning toward me. "You just learned why no one is ever going to steal the Black Papyrus on my watch. The entire mouseum is wired with an ULTRA-MODERN alarm system. It's super-efficient, super-intelligent, and recognizes every single suspicious movement. You've also just met the Toughtail siblings, four exceptionally well-trained guards. They won't let any mouse mess with the papyrus." He gestured at the guards surrounding me. "Now you may have your glasses back, Mr. Stilton," he said, handing them over.

Cheese and crackers — finally!

A Fancy Rodent

At that moment, we heard a strange noise. . . .

What was that?

I couldn't investigate because I was still surrounded by guards. (How ridiculous!) But there was definitely a strange noise coming from a nearby room. It sounded like the tip of an **umbrella** hitting the tiled floor, followed by a metallic tinkling. Rancid ricotta, what could it be?

Then a voice interrupted my thoughts. "Guards, stop — there must be a mistake!"

Ah-ha! I only knew one rodent who wore so much jewelry that she sounded like a

Hmm . . .
Stop!
Countess!

bazillion tiny bells when she moved. It was none other than the insanely wealthy Countess Cordelia Sparklepaws! She was one of the most refined rodents in New Mouse City. Every so often, I ran into her at FANCY exhibits and concerts.

She whirled into the room, waving her paws. "My dearest 00W, don't worry about Mr. Stilton — he wouldn't hurt a **FLY**!"

00W exclaimed, "But, Countess, he's suspicious. **Very, very suspicious!**"

The countess rolled her eyes. "Cheesy cream puffs, what do you really think this intellectual rodent is going to do? He's no thief — let him go!"

As soon as the guards backed away, I

approached the countess. "May I?" I asked, and **kissed her paw**. I'm a real gentlemouse!

As I looked up at her, I counted:

one dozen priceless bracelets,
a matching priceless necklace,
sparkling priceless earrings,
and a priceless diamond tiara!

Even the countess's clothes were woven with priceless gold and silver threads.

Chattering cheddar, what a fancy rodent!

The countess smiled. "Well, Mr. Stilton, you must be wondering why I'm here."

I nodded and scratched my snout thoughtfully. "Yes, actually, I am."

"I'm here to demand that the Black Papyrus be put up for auction," the countess announced. "I want the secret of eternal youth for myself. I intend to bid HIGH . . .

IDENTIFICATION CARD

First name: **Cordelia**
Last name: **Sparklepaws**
Who she is: **The richest rodent in all of Mouse Island!**
Her passion: **She collects art and artifacts that are one-of-a-kind. She'll do anything to get them!**
Her secret: **She has a horrible fear . . . of butterflies!**

I must have it!

so HIGH that no rodent can outbid me!"

She did a little twirl. "*I* must have the **BLACK PAPYRUS** — no one else!" she went on. "Once I uncover its secret, I'll never age. I'll always be **beautiful**! I can create an entire line of beauty products with my name on them. It will be fabumouse!"

"Countess, this all sounds a little **suspicious** to me," 00W remarked. "First, Mr. Stilton did a number of very suspicious things. And now you're starting to sound pretty suspicious yourself. I'm keeping an **EYE** on you!"

Super-Suspicious Rodents!

Somewhere behind us we suddenly heard a **sneeze** and then a **COUGH**.

OOW spun around. "Hey! Who coughed? Who sneezed?" he asked, as alert as a mouse in a cavern full of cats.

"Heh, heh, heh! That was me," a voice said. "Well, I **LAUGHED**!"

A short, stout, *well-dressed* rodent came forward. He had a pyramid-shaped gem on the lapel of his jacket, and a yellow daisy in the jacket's buttonhole. He bowed and introduced himself.

"My name is PETER PAPERTAIL, collector of ancient papyrus. I'm also an international expert on hieroglyphics. I've waited a long

time for the chance to decipher the **BLACK PAPYRUS**. Cheese niblets — according to legend, it holds the secret of eternal youth!" He LAUGHED again.

"Why are you LAUGHING?" I asked, twisting my whiskers in confusion. "What's so funny?"

"The countess says she plans to bid HIGH

IDENTIFICATION CARD

First name: **Peter**
Last name: **Papertail**
Who he is: **The most famouse papyrus collector on Mouse Island**
His hobby: **Deciphering papyruses and ancient hieroglyphics**
His secret: **During his free time, he participates in puzzle tournaments. He is also a sudoku champion!**

for the Black Papyrus?" he responded with a smirk. "Well, I'm going to bid even HIGHER! Mousetastically high!"

"You seem suspicious, too," 00W said darkly.

Papertail chuckled again. "Heh, heh, heh! Well, there's nothing I can do about that."

"Your answer is very suspicious," 00W went on. "And your LAUGH is suspicious, too. Besides, if you laughed before,

then who sneezed and coughed?"

"Achoo! It was me," a voice squeaked.

A short, stocky rodent with GRAY FUR and thick glasses perched on a long snout stepped out from behind a sarcophagus.

The mysterious mouse wore a white lab coat that was completely covered with STAINS. Test tubes and sheets of crumpled notebook paper spilled out of every pocket.

"Who are you?" 00W asked.

"Oh, I'm sorry!" the mouse said nervously.

"My name is **STEVE SWISSWHISKERS**, researcher and scientist. I . . . um . . . got **LOST**. I was looking for the bathroom! **Achoo!**"

After a loud sneeze, he continued, "I'm sorry, I'm allergic to dust. **Achoo!** By the way, I'm totally opposed to the idea of putting

First name: **Steve**
Last name: **Swisswhiskers**
Who he is: **A researcher and scientist, and a dean of science at Squeaksnout University.**
His passion: **He loves doing all kinds of experiments, but his true passion is searching for the secret of eternal youth.**
His secret: **He has a collection of ancient cheese rinds!**

the Black Papyrus up for auction. Its SECRET must be left to the scientists and used for the improvement of all mice everywhere! Achoo!"

OOW LOOKED the stuffy rodent up and down. Standing snout-to-snout with him, he concluded, "You're also suspicious. Very, very suspicious!"

Benjamin and Bugsy burst out laughing.

Hee, hee, hee!

"You can't suspect EVERYONE!" Thea said with a smile. "Nothing has even happened yet. The alarm only went off in the first place because of my cheesebrain of a brother!"

Just then, the alarm went off again — and this time, it was pawsitively not my fault!

A Not-So-False Alarm

The alarm was coming from my friend Professor Sandsnout's office! Holey mummified cheese! Was he in trouble?

"Hurry, let's CHECK IT OUT!" Thea exclaimed.

But 00W stopped her. "Don't move a whisker! This is a very DANGEROUS situation! I have to keep you all under surveillance!"

"But . . . but . . . my friend's in there!" I squeaked, twisting my tail into a knot. "Friendship is the most important thing in the world — even more important than the secret of the Black Papyrus!"

00W stared at me for a moment and then said, "ALL RIGHT, the Stilton family can come with me. That way, I can keep an EYE on your suspicious snouts!"

With the GUARDS leading the way, we entered Professor Sandsnout's office. Putrid cheese puffs — the professor was sprawled out on the floor, unconscious! Someone had KNOCKED him on the head!

One of the guards pointed his paw at a glass case. "Look — the Black Papyrus is gone!"

"I'm a dead mouse," 00W murmured, tugging his whiskers in PANIC. "How am I going to explain this to the mice at M.I.S.S.O.?"

Benjamin and I tried to revive the professor with Gorgonzola smelling salts. After a minute, he twitched his whiskers, blinked, and squeaked weakly, "What happened?"

"I'm the one asking the questions here! What happened?" exclaimed 00W. "This is awfully SUSPICIOUS, Professor! You were just sitting in your

office while the Black Papyrus disappeared, and you have no idea how it happened?"

Professor Sandsnout shook his head in confusion. "I heard something rustle behind me. I turned around to look — and someone HIT me square on the snout!"

"There's clearly a **thief** on the premises!" 00W cried.

"But how will we ever find him? He's probably long gone by now," Thea said.

"Impossible," 00W said confidently. "We

have an extremely sophisticated **alarm system**. No can get out of the mouseum without me knowing about it!"

Thea wasn't convinced. "But the **WINDOW** is open!"

Swiss cheese on rye — Thea was right!

OOW **walked over** to take a peek. "It seems like it's open, but . . . **LOOK**!"

He waved a paw toward the window, and a heavy metal **GATE** came clattering down. **Clang!**

What a fabumouse alarm system!

"No one can escape!" 00W proclaimed.

"What if they went out through the DOORS?" asked Benjamin.

"Nope." 00W shook his snout. "All of the mouseum's exits SLAM shut as soon as the alarm is triggered."

Rancid ricotta, that could mean only one thing! My whiskers trembled with fright, and I turned PALE.

I stammered, "TH-THAT MEANS THE TH-TH-THIEF IS STILL HERE — HIDDEN IN THE MOUSEUM!"

YOU'RE IN GOOD PAWS!

We'll search for clues!

"There's no time to *twiddle our tails*!" 00W exclaimed. "There's a mystery to solve! Geronimo may look like a **cheesebrain**, but he's right — the thief is still in the mouseum. This is a dangerous situation. Don't worry, I'm on the case. You're in good PAWS!"

He lowered his sunglasses and peered carefully at each one of us.

"We need to split up and search for CLUES. For your protection, each of you will be escorted by one of the Toughtails. I believe you've already met them."

Chattering cheddar — of course we'd met the Toughtails! They were the same guards who had surrounded me earlier!

"Believe me, the Toughtails are prepared for this CHALLENGE," 00W assured us.

Just then, a mouse with eyes as cold as ice came toward me and held out her paw. "Nice to meet you. I'm Tessa Toughtail."

Cheese and crackers, that rough and tough

rodent reminded me of someone. But who?

"Tony, Tom, Trevor — come here! Let's show them what we Toughtails are made of," Tessa called to her brothers.

Before I could blink, all four guards took off their jackets and started doing PUSH-UPS.

I was squeakless — they were so athletic!

"We're experts in all different kinds of martial arts," Tessa said. "We're SUPER-trained, SUPER-skilled, and SUPER-fit!" She paused and grinned. "I have an idea, Geronimo. Why don't you and I have a quick little martial arts competition?"

Was this mouse out of her mind?

"Uh . . . actually . . ." I began slowly.

Luckily, Thea stepped in. I can always count on my sister to help me out of a sticky situation!

She turned to Tessa. "I'm a **MARTIAL ARTS** champion. I'd be happy to challenge you."

Tessa Toughtail GRINNED. "I accept!"

The Toughtail brothers suddenly appeared with a pile of WOODEN BOARDS. Tessa took three, stacked them on top of one another, chopped with her paw, and shouted, "**HIIIYA!**" The boards fell to the floor, **broken** cleanly in half. Slimy Swiss cheese!

But Thea's **FUR** wasn't ruffled. She smiled and grabbed SIX BOARDS! She calmly stacked them and broke them with a quick CHOP. My sister was one muscular mouse!

The tradition of breaking boards, blocks, or tiles is called TAMESHIWARI in Japanese. This tradition is common in many martial arts. It can only be done by skilled athletes, so don't try it at home! You could hurt yourself!

"Can you do better

than that, Miss Toughtail?" Thea said, a smile stretching across her snout.

Tessa ROLLED her icy eyes, stacked EIGHT boards, and broke them with one paw. (She reminded me of someone . . . but who?)

Thea stacked TEN boards and broke them with one elbow.

Tessa stacked TWELVE boards and broke them with one fist.

Thea stacked TWENTY boards and broke them with one kick.

Tessa stacked THIRTY boards, sneered at me, raised her paws . . . and BOPPED me right in the snout with her elbow!

CRUSTY CAT LITTER — I BLACKED OUT!

A MATCHUP BETWEEN TWO MIGHTY MICE

5
Tessa broke twelve with one fist!
6
Thea broke twenty with a flying kick!
And now . . .
7
Tessa stacked thirty, raised her paws, and . . . hit me square in the snout!

AN IMPORTANT CLUE

This time, Professor Sandsnout helped me, instead of the other way around! He revived me with the GORGONZOLA smelling salts. Oof, what an unfortunate accident! In the meantime, 00W was carefully checking the display case that had held the BLACK PAPYRUS.

"Bad news," he said, shaking his snout. "The MACHINE the professor invented to unroll the papyrus is also gone."

"Moldy mozzarella!" I cried, jumping to my paws. "That means the **thief** can unroll the papyrus without harming it — and uncover its secret!"

00W grumbled, "Mr. Stilton, sometimes

you're awfully smart. I have to say, it's very suspicious!"

Oh, cheese and crackers — this rodent was starting to get on my nerves!

"Uncle G," Benjamin called just then. "LOOK — there's something back here!"

I joined my nephew and saw that there was a small yellow object behind the display case. 00W picked up the evidence with a pair of tweezers and placed it inside a plastic envelope. It was a yellow FLOWER PETAL!

HOW STRANGE!

00W looked at me and said, "Hmm . . . this petal is definitely important evidence! Mr. Stilton, could you have fainted on purpose as a distraction, to keep us from finding this evidence? I think it's about time I gave you my SUPER-DUPER TRUTH TEST!"

Cheese niblets, was he serious?!

Professor Sandsnout quickly held up a paw. "It's ridiculous to suspect Geronimo Stilton!"

00W shushed him. "I suspect EVERYTHING and EVERYONE!"

"I understand that," the professor said with a sigh. "But Geronimo is my dear friend, and I trust him completely!"

"I don't even trust my own SHADOW," 00W said proudly.

For some reason, the Toughtails gasped at that. HOW STRANGE!

"No matter who took the papyrus," Professor Sandsnout said, "they won't understand what's written on it without my help — even if they do manage to unroll it

with my MACHINE. I'm the only mouse who can translate it!"

Cheesy cream puffs — that meant Professor Sandsnout was still in **DANGER**! Sooner or later, the papyrus thief would figure out that he needed the professor's help. Then they'd mousenap him!

We had to do something to protect him!

00W agreed. "Professor Sandsnout, you're in an enormouse amount of **DANGER**! From now on, we'll take turns making sure nothing happens to you. I'll stay here with Thea during the day, and Mr. Stilton and the Toughtails will spend the NIGHT in the mouseum with you."

Spending the night in the mouseum? Squeak! I couldn't think of anything more FUR-RAISING!

Just thinking about the MUMMIES . . .

the SARCOPHAGI . . .

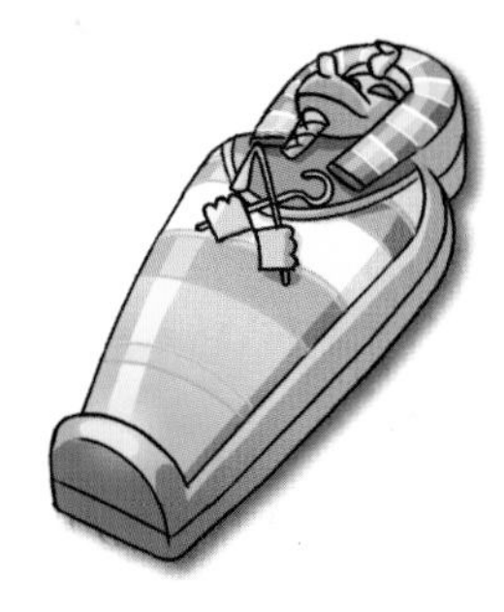

the **thief** lurking somewhere in the dark hallways . . .

I fainted again!

A Night in the Mouseum

The thought of spending an entire NIGHT in the mouseum made my fur stand on end! But the professor needed my help — I couldn't BACK OUT on him.

OOW grumbled, "Get a GRIP, Geronimo! We have to investigate, INSPECT, and analyze! Go home, and come back at DUSK when it's your turn to keep watch."

I shuddered.

"Don't worry — the professor and the Toughtails will be here with you," OOW went on. "They'll follow you

around like a SHADOW!"

Just then, one of the guards gasped again. HOW STRANGE! Though maybe spending so much time with 00W was making me super-suspicious . . .

For now, Benjamin, Bugsy, and I left the MOUSEUM. 00W had asked PETER PAPERTAIL, STEVE SWISSWHISKERS, and Countess Sparklepaws to go home and return the following morning, so they left with us, too. By now, there wasn't a single rodent lined up outside! When word got out that the BLACK PAPYRUS was stolen, everyone had hightailed it out of there.

I wondered: Would we find the papyrus?

I wondered: Would we uncover its

mysterious secret?

I wondered: Would we live to see tomorrow? Squeak!

My whiskers were wobbling as I said good-bye to Bugsy and Benjamin and headed to the office. I tried to put my snout down, work hard, and not think about the night ahead!

At NIGHTFALL, I stood outside the

entrance of the mouseum again. I knocked until **OOW** himself opened the door.

"Come in, Geronimo! It's your turn — but remember, this could be very dangerous! Try not to mess it up. Just in case, you do have a will, right?"

DANGEROUS?
MESS UP?
WILL?
ACK! I WAS FRIGHTENED OUT OF MY FUR!

I headed toward Professor Sandsnout's office by myself, twisting my tail in knots. As I CLIMBED the stairs, it felt like someone was following me! When I finally entered the Hall of Sarcophagi, I heard a **STRANGE** creaking noise. Rotten rat's teeth — were the lids of the sarcophagi OPENING?!

I chewed my whiskers in terror, threw open the office door, and . . .

Professor?!

I found the professor lying flat on the floor. He was out cold!

Double twisted rat tails! The professor had been left alone, and someone had knocked him out! Maybe that someone had meant to mousenap him — and had run out of time!

I had to get my tail in gear and do something quick, BUT WHAT? The professor was unconscious, and I was alone at NIGHT in the mouseum! I needed help!

I squeaked at the top of my lungs:

"HELP! HELP! HELP! HELP! HELP! HELP! HEL

HELP! HELP! HELP! HELP! HELP! HELP! HELP! HELP! HELP! HELP! HELP! HELP!

HELP! HELP! HELP! HELP! HELP! HELP! HELP! HELP! HELP! HELP! HELP! HELP!

HELP! HELP! HELP! HELP! HELP! HELP! HELP! HELP! HELP! HELP! HELP! HELP!

HELP! HELP! HELP! HELP! HELP! HELP! HELP! HELP! HELP! HELP! HELP! HELP!

I pulled out my cell phone and was about to call 00W when I heard another noise. I spun around in a panic. Holey cheese — four MUMMIES stood behind me! They were wrapped in bandages from the ends of their ears to the tips of their tails. Before I could squeak, the shortest mummy came toward me, gave me an icy-cold LOOK with its blue eyes, and bonked me on the head. I went out like a light!

A Familiar Fragrance

My mind was racing with thoughts of bandages, mummies, and blue eyes when I suddenly whiffed something familiar — GORGONZOLA smelling salts!

Lucky for me, Thea, Benjamin, and Bugsy Wugsy had come to my rescue just in time!

I OPENED my eyes and asked, "What happened? What are you all doing here?"

"You passed out, Uncle G!" Bugsy explained.

"We knew you didn't like the idea of being **alone** in the mouseum," Benjamin added. "So Aunt Thea, Bugsy, and I hid in the HALL OF SARCOPHAGI and waited for you to show up. We wanted to **SURPRISE** you!"

"Then we heard a strange noise coming from the professor's office — and here we are," Thea finished.

I had the most fabumouse family!

I tried to get up on my paws, but another strange noise rang out in the hall. My poor paws went limp, like string cheese left out in the sun!

"Cheese niblets, we're in DANGER!" I told Thea, Benjamin, and Bugsy. "A few minutes ago, four mummies appeared behind me and KNOCKED me out cold! I think they had done the same thing to Professor Sandsnout . . ."

Holey moldy cheese — wait! Where was the professor? He had been lying on the floor only moments earlier . . . but he had vanished when I wasn't looking!

Whiskers wobbling with fear, I squeaked, "I think the mummies mousenapped the professor! I could tear out my whiskers — I came here to protect him, and now he's GONE!"

"He can't be too FAR, Mr. Stilton," said 00W, appearing behind me. "Don't worry! All of the mouseum exits are protected by my super-duper high-tech

security system. No one is getting out of here, so we have time for you to take my little **TEST**, Mr. Stilton!"

"Slimy Swiss cheese!" I yelped. "Me?! **WHY?**"

"Because you're suspicious!" 00W said. Ugh, I should have known! "Your story about the mummies stinks more than **GOOEY GORGONZOLA**! To get to the bottom of this,

I'm going to give you a test with my very own fabumouse TRUTH MACHINE."

He held up a strange-looking helmet covered with WIRES.

"I call the machine VERITAS," he said. "It's never made a mistake!"

The Moment of Truth

I agreed to put on the helmet connecting me to Veritas, the TRUTH MACHINE. I had nothing to hide, and maybe 00W would finally stop suspecting me once I passed his test!

Cheese niblets — that helmet was HEAVY!

"Answer all my questions honestly," 00W warned me. "When we're done, we'll know for sure if you're a suspicious squeaker or just an ordinary 'FRAIDY MOUSE!"

This rodent was really starting to get UNDER MY FUR! But I sighed and answered, "All right . . ."

00W didn't waste any time. "What did you see when you ENTERED this room tonight?"

"I saw my friend Professor Sandsnout lying unconscious on the floor," I replied, shivering at the memory. "And in that corner there were four MUMMIES!"

"MUMMIES? On the floor?" he asked.

I shook my snout. "No! The mummies were standing and moving — TOWARD ME!"

"That sounds awfully suspicious," 00W said with narrowed eyes.

RATS! Would I ever be able to convince him I wasn't a suspicious rodent?

As I was answering questions, the guards

came in and surrounded me.

"Okay," 00W continued, "I'm going to question you until there's not a SHADOW of a doubt that you're telling the truth!"

I was sure that I heard the guards gasp this time. HOW STRANGE!

00W didn't seem to notice anything. "Now, do you normally go around carrying YELLOW FLOWER PETALS?"

"No!" I shook my snout. "That isn't mine!"

"Hmm . . . are you aware that the guards found another CLUE?"

00W held up a piece of BROKEN GLASS. "Tell the truth! Is this yours?"

"No!" I said confidently. "I've never seen that before in my life. Rodent's honor!"

"Remember, my TRUTH MACHINE will catch you if you lie, Mr. Stilton!" 00W said. He glanced down at the floor and stopped in his tracks. "Look! Another CLUE!"

00W bent down and picked up a diamond earring!

"Is this piece of jewelry yours?"

"It's not mine!" I hollered. I was getting awfully tired of this cheddar-headed mouse suspecting me of everything!

00W shook his snout. "Veritas will analyze your answers to determine if you told me the truth. We'll finally know if you're

It wasn't meeeee!

guilty of stealing the Black Papyrus!"

The machine hummed and buzzed, then spit out a small piece of PAPER. 00W peered at it carefully. His eyes widened in surprise, then drooped in disappointment. "Hmm. Veritas says you told the truth. You're innocent!" He twisted his tail sheepishly. "Maybe I'm a little too suspicious sometimes. Could you forgive me, Mr. Stilton?"

I smiled and held out my paw, relieved.

Who Stole the Black Papyrus?

The helmet on my head felt **HEAVIER** than a twenty-pound wheel of cheese! As I struggled to take it off, 00W asked, "Mr. Stilton, who do you think stole the **BLACK PAPYRUS**? Let's work together to come up with a suspect."

I finally stopped trying to take off the helmet, and **paused** to think.

"We found a yellow petal," I said slowly. "It could belong to PETER PAPERTAIL — he had a flower in his buttonhole! But that's not proof that he stole the papyrus. He could have lost the flower anytime he was in the mouseum."

00W nodded. "Right! It would be STRANGE

for a criminal to leave such an obvious piece of evidence."

"The diamond earring could belong to Countess Sparklepaws," I mused. "But someone could have put it there on purpose to frame her!"

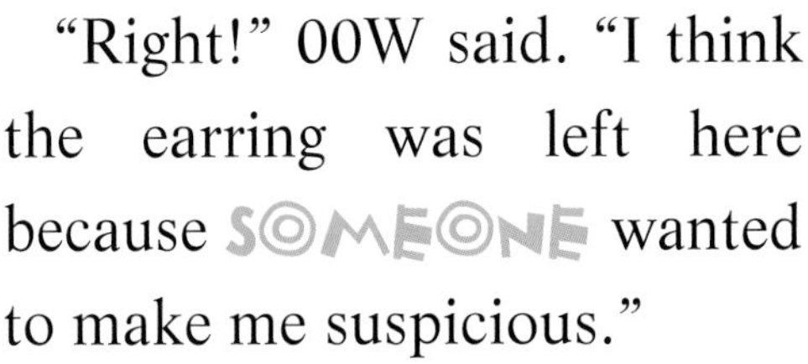

"Right!" 00W said. "I think the earring was left here because SOMEONE wanted to make me suspicious."

"And the piece of glass," I continued, "looks like the bottom of a test tube. That makes me think of STEVE SWISSWHISKERS. But somebody could have planted it to throw us off track."

00W looked at me with a grin. "Right again! I knew I could trust you — you figured

everything out!"

Huh? I HADN'T FIGURED OUT A THING! "Um, who do you think it was?" I asked.

OOW shrugged. "I have no clue. You tell me, Mr. Stilton . . ."

This OOW was one **frustrating** mouse!

In the meantime, the truth helmet had become enormousely heavy. Plus, I had a TERRIBLE ITCH on my head. I tried to move the helmet to the right. Then I tried to move the helmet to the left. But I felt like tearing out my whiskers. It was stuck!

I put my snout down and pulled and pulled on the helmet with both paws. It finally came off with a pop — and flew all the way across the room! I tried to catch it, but I wasn't fast enough and it hit a sarcophagus. RATS! Before I could wiggle a whisker, the sarcophagus began to WOBBLE . . . and TILT . . . and then it FELL right on top of one of the guards!

The guard staggered and fell on top of another guard, who fell on top of the third guard, who bumped right into Tessa

Toughtail! As she tumbled to the floor, something **FELL** out of her suit.

HOW STRANGE!

OOW scurried toward the guards and suddenly spotted another earring on the floor, three **YELLOW FLOWER PETALS**, another broken test tube, and some bandages.

What could it all mean?

"This is *very suspicious*!" 00W said. "Did someone plant these clues to trick me? MAYBE someone dressed up like a mummy . . . and MAYBE this isn't really a guard's uniform. It's a disguise!" he concluded.

As quickly as a mouse snatching the last morsel of cheese off a platter, 00W peeled off Tessa Toughtail's disguise. Putrid cheese puffs, that wasn't Tessa Toughtail! It was the SHADOW — the most notorious thief in all of Mouse Island!

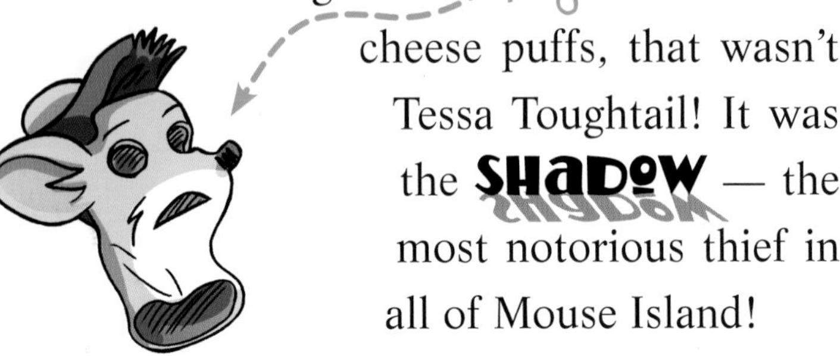

THAT'S WHY I RECOGNIZED THOSE ICY-BLUE EYES!

This is a disguise!

THE SHADOW IN FLIGHT

THE SHADOW looked at me and laughed. "Geronimo, I'm disappointed! Didn't you recognize me?" She smoothed her long blonde hair. "Did you really think we were guards? Ha! You all fell for our trick! But even better — you didn't CATCH us!"

What?!

She threw a can to the floor, and the room immediately filled with thick smoke.

While we were enveloped in smoke, we heard the sound of hurried pawsteps scurrying off . . .

OOW HOLLERED, "Hurry, they're getting away! We have to catch them and find out

TOP-SECRET

The Shadow

Who she is: **Sally Ratmousen's cousin.**

Profession: **The most notorious thief on Mouse Island! She'll do absolutely anything to get rich.**

Fun facts: **As a master of disguise, the Shadow knows every trick in the book—she's an expert at completing her robberies totally undetected.**

Strength: **The Shadow always disguises herself in different, creative ways—but under every disguise, she wears her signature black outfit.**

Weakness: **Every time she encounters Geronimo Stilton, her robberies fail!**

where they hid the **BLACK PAPYRUS**. But more importantly, we have to find out where they took Professor Sandsnout!"

I began to run, but **I couldn't see a cheese crumb** through all the smoke!

Thea was right behind me. "**MOVE**, Geronimo! Run! Run!"

The Shadow turned and burst out laughing. "Catch me if you can, **cheesebrains**!"

I DASHED through the halls of the mouseum as fast as my paws would carry me.

I ran and ran until I tripped on an urn, lost my balance, and TUMBLED down the stairs. I bounced on every single step — YOUCH! — until I slammed into a priceless Egyptian sarcophagus at the bottom. I was just in time to spot the Shadow and her accomplices fleeing through a trapdoor.

Heeeeeelp!

When I GOT UP, my tail ached and my paws were as wobbly as string cheese! But I kept running as if my tail were on FIRE — I had to catch the Shadow. As I ran, I noticed that the lid of one of the sarcophagi was slowly lifting. Rotten rat's teeth, how CREEPY! Even worse, I could see two eyes staring out at me . . . and then a PAW poked out of the sarcophagus!

HOLEY CHEESE . . . I WAS TERRIFIED!

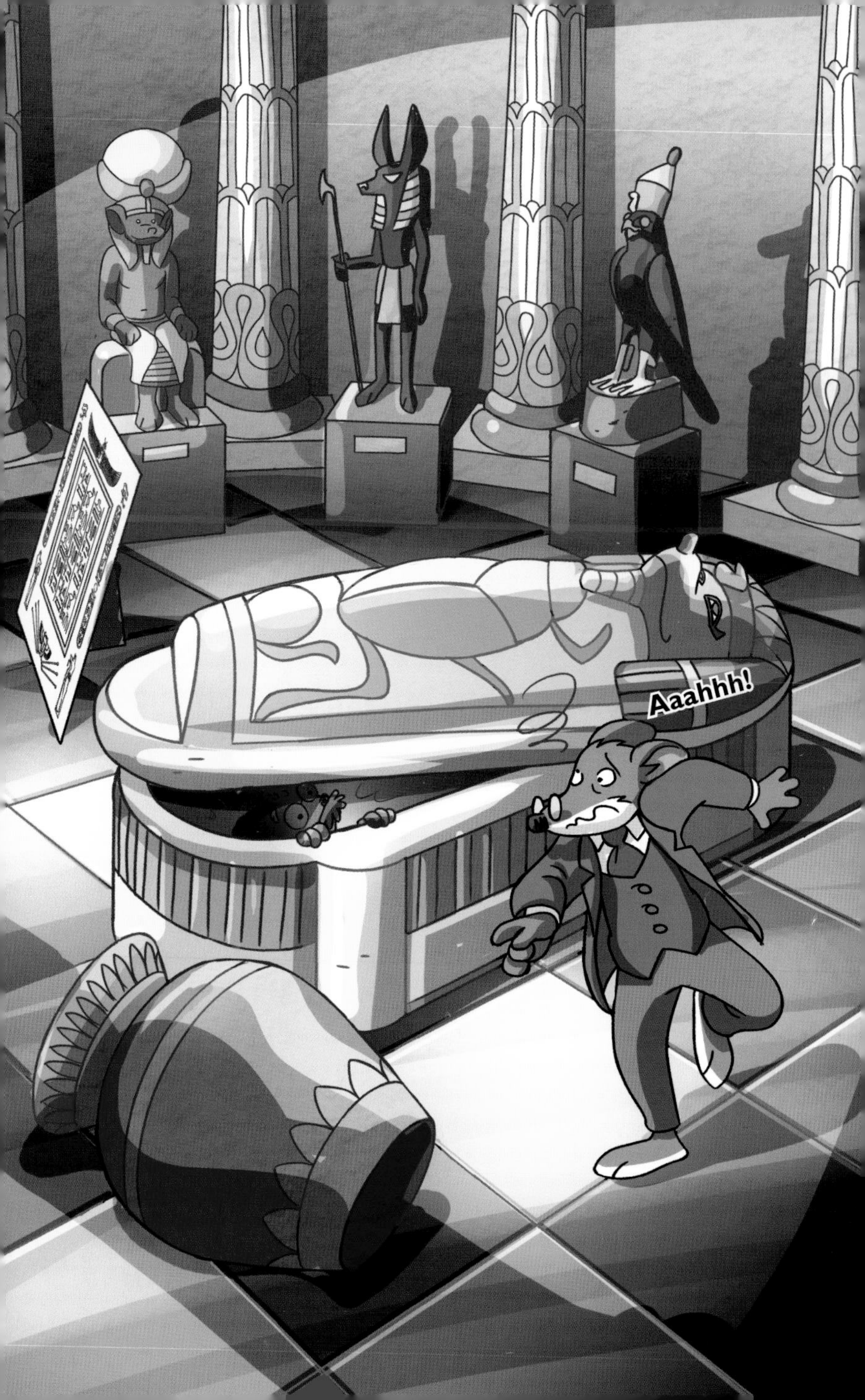
Aaahhh!

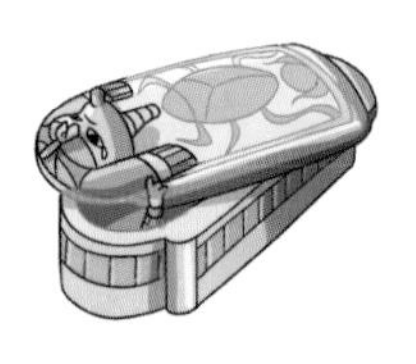

SARCOPHAGUS SURPRISE!

The paw moved, as if asking for help. But I couldn't help — I had already fainted with fright!

While Thea REVIVED me with Gorgonzola smelling salts (again!), Benjamin and Bugsy opened the sarcophagus.

Mummified mozzarella — Professor Sandsnout was inside! He was a bit dazed and a little BRUISED, but a huge smile crossed his snout when he saw us. He climbed out and hugged each of us tightly.

Then he revealed some marvemouse news — the thieves may have gotten away, but they were empty-pawed. They didn't take the BLACK PAPYRUS or the SPECIAL MACHINE to unroll it. Instead, they had locked them in the sarcophagus with Professor Sandsnout! Maybe the thieves had planned to come back for them some other time when no one was on their tails, but luckily, we found them first.

00W asked, "How are you feeling, Professor?"

Professor Sandsnout sighed. "My paws ACHE, my tail is numb, and I feel dizzy!"

Then he chuckled. "Fortunately, I had this FLASHLIGHT on me, or I would have been really bored."

What in the name of CHEESE did he mean?

"I realized that the BLACK PAPYRUS was also inside the sarcophagus," the professor explained. "So . . . I unrolled it with my machine and deciphered it!"

I was stunned.

"Cheese and crackers," I whispered. "Professor, you mean to tell us that you've discovered the secret of the Black Papyrus?"

Professor Sandsnout grinned. "Well, I had NOTHING ELSE to do in the sarcophagus!"

I couldn't believe my ears.

"Professor, you're a HERO!" I exclaimed.

00W walked over, took off his dark glasses, and said, "I see two HEROES here! Fabumouse work, Geronimo. Without you, we could have LOST the Black Papyrus for good!" Then he whispered, "My cousin 00K was right — you may look like a cheesebrain, but you're an excellent sleuth, Agent 00G!"

I blushed.

00W turned to Professor Sandsnout. "Hey, Professor, want to tell us the secret of the Black Papyrus?" he asked.

The professor cleared his throat and solemnly read the scroll aloud:

The secret of staying young is to live every day filled with joy and to appreciate everything around you!

Where do I put this?
Here!
Fabumouse work, Stilton!

Cheese niblets, how **wise**!

00W didn't give us a chance to reflect on the secret before he shouted, "No time to waste — everybody back to work! The exhibition is opening tomorrow, and everything's a mousely MESS!"

Within a few hours, all traces of the Shadow had been erased. The **BLACK PAPYRUS** was returned to its display case, and everything else was back in place, too. We were all pawsitively exhausted!

GERONIMOOOO!

I said good-bye and finally headed home on dragging paws. I couldn't wait to get some rest! But as soon as I walked through the door, the phone rang. It was Grandfather William.

Putrid cheese puffs, this wasn't going to be good!

"Geronimo! What are you doing home? Why aren't you in the office?" he **THUNDERED**.

"Actually, I was just about to go to bed —" I started.

"**WHAAAAAT?**" he bellowed. "Do you want *The Rodent's Gazette* to become a horrible failure?"

I tried to calm him down, but he hollered, "You have to write your **article** about the Black Papyrus now, before some other rodent beats you to it! Explain everything you've discovered in minute detail!"

My whiskers drooped. I was so tired . . . but Grandfather William was right. So I scampered to the **OFFICE** to write all about the secret of the Black Papyrus.

THE RODENT'S GAZETTE

The most famouse newspaper on Mouse Island

REVEALED: THE SECRET OF THE BLACK PAPYRUS

The text of the Black Papyrus has been deciphered!

Do you want to know the secret of the Black Papyrus and eternal youth? Easy: Live every day filled with joy and appreciate everything around you. It's a simple but important rule!

See page 3 for Geronimo Stilton's editorial:

THE MYSTERIOUS FORMULA FOR ETERNAL YOUTH

Yesterday was an enormousely significant day at the Egyptian Mouseum in New Mouse City. For a whisker-twitching moment, we feared we had lost a priceless treasure — the famouse Black Papyrus. Fortunately, thanks to Secret Agent 00W, the ancient papyrus was quickly found . . . unharmed!

In a fur-raising twist, Professor Cyril B. Sandsnout, director of the Egyptian Mouseum, was mouse-napped and held in a sarcophagus! But while in captivity, Sandsnout was able to finish translating the Black Papyrus. The professor has finally revealed the secret of eternal youth: Live life with joy!

THE SECRET OF THE BLACK PAPYRUS

We sold thousands and thousands of copies of that edition of the *Gazette*. The secret of the **BLACK PAPYRUS** was a fabumouse lesson for everyone!

The first rodent to come thank me was Countess Sparklepaws. "Oh, Geronimo! To think I wanted to keep that secret all to myself. The best way to stay young is to live each day to the fullest! With generosity! Because of this, dear Geronimo, I've decided to take all the money I was going to use to buy the papyrus and donate it to charity. What do you think?"

"I think that's a marvemouse idea, Countess!" I exclaimed. "You are truly a mousetastic rodent."

You surprised me!

Then PETER PAPERTAIL paid me a visit. "Geronimo, you surprised me!" he said. "I thought I knew everything about the ANCIENT EGYPTIANS, but you reminded me that a rodent never stops learning. THANK YOU!"

STEVE SWISSWHISKERS came to see me, too. "To be young on the inside is the real secret. How wonderful! Thanks, Geronimo!"

Thank you!

By the time I got home, I knew for sure that the secret of the Black Papyrus was one of those special secrets that's better when **EVERYONE** knows about it!

Here's a copy of the paper!
The secret is revealed!
Are you done?
Hmm . . .

Everyone back to work!
Thank you, friends!

And that's the reason I write, and will keep writing every day — in order to appreciate everything around me! But I also write to help myself recognize what TRULY matters in life: friendship, family, love, peace, nature . . .

Dear rodent friends, always remember that

That's the truth — rodent's honor — or my name isn't *Geronimo Stilton*!

Dear readers,

The Black Papyrus taught me to appreciate everything in my life! On a separate sheet of paper, try writing down your answers to these questions. Just thinking about such wonderful things will make you feel fabumouse!

What's really important to you?

Who are the most significant people (or rodents!) in your life?

What makes you happiest?

Now check out this bonus
Mini Mystery story!
Join me in solving a whisker-licking-good mystery. Find clues along with me as you read. Together, we'll be super-squeaky investigators!

THE CAT GANG

Bills, Bills, and More Bills!

It was a bright **Fall** day. It was the kind of day that makes a mouse want to stop **scampering** and just breathe.

From the window of my office, I stared out at the **colorful** leaves and sniffed the crisp air. Ah . . .

If only I could shut out the sounds of the bustling **newsroom** behind me. What newsroom? Oh, excuse me! I haven't introduced myself. My name is Stilton, *Geronimo Stilton*, and I run *The Rodent's Gazette*, the most famouse newspaper on Mouse Island.

Dwayne Digitpaws, the financial manager, began squeaking in my ear.

"Mr. Stilton! We need to go over the monthly **bills**!" he insisted.

Bills, bills, and more bills! If there's one thing I can't stand, it's dealing with the monthly **bills**.

I tried to convince Dwayne to talk to me after lunch, but it was as if his ears were **stuffed** with cheese. He kept on squeaking.

"**LOOK** here, Mr. Stilton," he said. "This month's phone bill is **$4,500**! And the cost of paper is ridiculous! We spent **$30,000**! And the new photocopier cost **$7,000**!"

There was no way to stop him. So I spent the whole morning going over the numbers and paying bills.

Sigh!

So much for my relaxing Fall morning.

Finally, Dwayne told me I needed to sign some documents over at the BANK.

"No problem," I agreed, heading for the door. I decided I would stop at home for lunch first. At least it would be peaceful there.

But I was wrong. . . .

SMILE, MR. STILTON!

As soon as I left *The Rodent's Gazette*, someone blinded me with a flash, yelling, "Nice shot, Mr. Stilton!"

I recognized him immediately. "Aren't you **Red Paparatz**, the photographer for the famouse, **scandalous** newspaper *Chatter*?" I asked.

"Exactly, Mr. Stilton!" answered Red, SNAPPING another picture. "Smile!"

I scratched my head. "Um, why are you taking my photo?" I mumbled as I was blinded by another series of flashes.

"I'm photographing you because I want to work for you!" replied Red. "I'll show you how good I am. Smile, please!"

By now I was starting to see STARS from all that flashing light.

"Please stop!" I wailed.

But Red kept snapping away.

"I'll stop when you hire me to work for your newspaper!" he demanded.

Luckily, I had just arrived in front of my house. "Ahem, I — I — I need to think about it, **Red**," I stammered. "I'll let you know as soon as I can."

Then I flung open the door and raced inside.

I was safe at last!

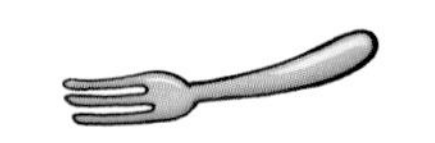

Flash! Flash!

To recover from my stressful morning, I treated myself to a delicious lunch of macaroni and cheese, mozzarella rolls, and **chocolate**-covered cheddar logs.

After lunch, I lay down for a quick mouse nap. I was awakened by the

sound of the telephone ringing.

It was Dwayne Digitpaws.

"Mr. Stilton!" he shrieked. "What are you still doing at home? The bank closes in fifteen minutes!"

Cheese niblets! I had forgotten all about going to the bank!

I left right away, but just outside my door stood an annoying surprise: Red Paparatz with his flashing camera!

"So, Mr. Stilton, will you hire me?" he asked as he followed me.

"Not now, Red," I muttered, racing along. "I'm in a hurry. I have to get to the bank."

But that didn't stop Red.

"Perfect!" he squeaked. "I can take some ACTION shots of you!"

I was running so fast, I was almost hit by a black van. It roared past me and screeched to a stop in front of the bank.

Meanwhile, **Red Paparatz** was clicking away.

Four Mysterious Mice

Four rodents wearing **dark** raincoats and **serious** expressions climbed out of the van. They headed into the bank.

But when I tried to follow them inside a moment later, the door was **locked**!

"Sour Swiss rolls!" I exclaimed. How strange! Those rodents had scampered inside just ahead of me.

Oh, well. At least **Red Paparatz** had stopped taking my picture and was taking shots of the bank instead.

Quiet as a mouse, I snuck back home. When I arrived, the phone rang. It was my sister, Thea.

"There was a robbery at the Bank of New Mouse City!" she said. "I'll meet you at the office!"

Rancid rat poison!

"But I was just there a half hour ago!" I cried.

I hung up the phone and turned on the TV. A newscaster was interviewing a bank teller.

"Did you see how many there were?" she asked.

"There were four, all dressed in BLACK," replied the teller. "Then an ENORMOUSE cat appeared."

"A cat?" asked the newscaster. "Are you sure?"

"Absolutely!" the teller replied. "It was the most **frightening** cat I've ever seen!"

I shuddered. An enormouse cat was TERRORIZING the rodents of New Mouse City! I was scared out of my fur, but I needed to get the story for the paper. If only we had pictures. Then I remembered Red Paparatz. He had photographed everything! I had to find him!

I'M INTO CLOSE-UPS

I opened my front door to search for Red Paparatz and was blinded by a FLASH! He had found me! We went to the newsroom together and Red downloaded more than two hundred photos onto Thea's computer. Too bad they were all terrible.

"Do you like my style, Mr. Stilton?" Red asked. "I'm into CLOSE-UPS."

I tried not to cry. There were shots of my nose, my paw, and my whiskers. Finally, an image appeared on the screen. It showed all FOUR VILLAINS putting the money into the van.

"How strange," commented Thea. "Someone is missing. It doesn't add up. . . ."

CLUE 1

Why does Thea Stilton say that it doesn't add up?

OOPS!

The following morning, I woke to the sound of the phone ringing.

"Hello?" I squeaked.

It was Dwayne Digitpaws.

"Did you go to the bank?" he asked.

Oops! I forgot again!

"I'm on my way to the **BANK OF NEW MOUSE CITY** right now!"

"Not that bank, Mr. Stilton!" he said with a sigh. "The papers are at the

Rodent Savings Bank!"

What?! I had gone to the **wrong** bank the previous day.

Just then, the doorbell rang.

It was my nephew **Benjamin** and his friend **Bugsy Wugsy**.

"Hi, Uncle Geronimo!" my nephew squeaked. "Guess what? It's a school holiday. Can we hang out with you?"

I gave Benjamin a huge hug. Oh, how I love that little mouse!

"Of course, my dear nephew," I said. "But first we need to take a quick trip to the bank. Then we'll go to my office. Sound good?"

"Yes!" Benjamin and Bugsy exclaimed.

A few minutes later we reached the bank. I couldn't believe my eyes.

CLUE 2

Look at the illustration on the next page. What does Geronimo see that is so surprising?

RODENT
SAVINGS BANK

THE BLACK VAN . . . AGAIN!

Sour Swiss rolls! The black van that I had seen yesterday was parked in front of the bank . . . again!

I turned as WHITE as a slice of mozzarella.

A minute later, a bright flash blinded me. Can you guess who was taking my picture?

It was **Red Paparatz**, of course!

"Not today, Red . . ." I began to tell him.

Then suddenly, four rodents dressed in **BLACK** sprang from the van.

Red tried to take a picture, but the smallest rodent SWIPED the camera. Then we were all shoved into the bank.

I gulped. Something told me these rodents were up to no good!

The One, the Only, the Incredible Cat-Cat!

As soon as we were inside, the biggest rodent immediately disconnected the bank surveillance camera.

"Hello, everyone!" the smallest rodent

squeaked. "I'd like you all to meet the one, the only, the incredible **Cat-Cat**!"

An enormouse cat appeared right before our eyes.

WHAT A SCARY FELINE!

"Cat-Cat will obey all my orders," the smallest rodent, who seemed to be the leader, continued. "I'd advise you to do as I say if you don't want to become cat **kibble**!"

Benjamin squeezed my paw tightly in fear. I tried not to scream. Holey cheese, that little mouse has some **grip**!

Meanwhile, the smallest rodent had turned to the bank manager, Martin Moneywhiskers.

"Open the safe, Moneybags," the robber demanded.

"It's Moneywhiskers," grumbled the manager. He led the robbers to the safe. The giant cat followed, claws SCREECHING against the marble floor.

UGH! How I hated that sound! It reminded me of PAWNAILS on a chalkboard. Cat-Cat really needed to find himself a giant nail file or a cat salon.

I was so busy thinking about nails, I didn't see Moneywhiskers hit a RED button on the wall. Within seconds, STEEL bars shot up from the floor.

The bars created a barrier between the robbers and the rest of us.

What a fabumouse antitheft system!

Forget the Fish Sandwich!

Everyone cheered. Well, except for the bank robbers. The gang kept **piling** money from the safe into laundry sacks. And then the **strangest** thing happened . . .

The leader of the robbers ordered Cat-Cat to **advance**. And to our amazement, he did!

Cat-Cat walked through the **STEEL** bars as if they were *invisible*!

He towered over Moneywhiskers with his teeth bared.

Oh, what a **fur-raising sight**!

"Your tricks won't work with us, Moneybags!" the little robber squeaked. "Now, if you hit any more buttons, I'm going to tell Cat-Cat to forget the fish sandwich he packed for lunch and EAT you instead! It's up to you!"

The manager held up his paws in defeat.

Then the four robbers left the bank with the money, and the big cat disappeared into thin air, exactly as he had appeared.

It was strange.

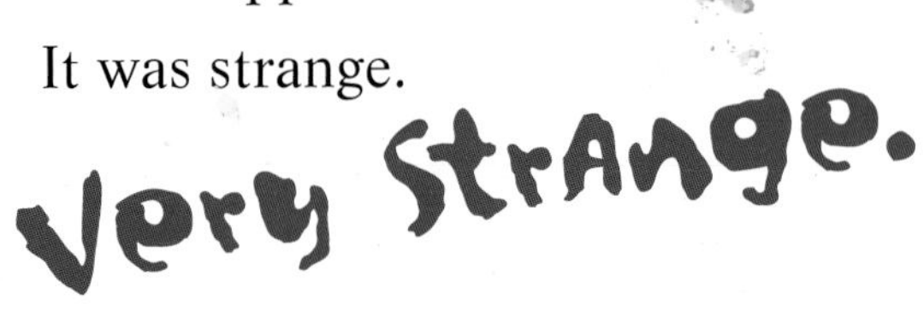

I'd like to **FILL** you in on what **happened** next, but I can't. That's because as soon as the **ROBBERS** left, I *fainted!*

Another Big Scoop!

When I opened my **eyes**, I found myself in my office.

"Wake up, Uncle Geronimo!" said my nephew Benjamin. "You're okay."

"Quit **NaPPiNG**, Gerry Berry," said my sister, Thea. "We've got a story to work on!"

"Check out the photo I took, Mr. Stilton!" That was Red Paparatz.

Photo?

I bolted upright.

"How did you get a picture without your camera?" I asked Red.

"Resourcefulness, Mr. Stilton!" he replied. "I carry a digital **micro-camera** in my hair at all times!"

Red showed me the images.

"But these are pictures of the CEILING and the inside of your ear," I observed.

"Oops," said Red, snatching back the photos and FLIPPING through them. "Here it is!"

He held up a blurry photo. It showed the back of the giant cat.

"Can we publish it?" Red squeaked.

The next day, the photo was on the front page of *The Rodent's Gazette*. The paper sold like freshly baked cheese Danish at The Pastry Rat.

"There's something strange about that photo," Benjamin said. "Look at the cat!"

17 Swiss Cheese Center
New Mouse City
Geronimo Stilton, Publisher
www.geronimostilton.com
The Rodent's Gazette
THE CAT GANG
STRIKES AGAIN

"Of course, Uncle G!" exclaimed Bugsy. "Look at the cat!"

"Right, the cat," I mumbled, though I had no idea what they were squeaking about.

CLUE 3

Do you notice something strange about the cat in Red Paparatz's photo?

G-G-G-Good Kitty!

"If there's no shadow . . ." said Bugsy.

"And it's TRANSPARENT . . ." added Benjamin.

"The only possible conclusion . . ." added Thea.

"Is that the cat is a g-g-ghost!" I stammered, feeling faint again.

Benjamin giggled. "No, Uncle, the conclusion is that the cat is a FAKE!"

"Now we just have to figure out how the ROBBERS make the cat appear," Bugsy said.

"A **FAKE**, of course." I coughed, pretending I knew what that meant. Lucky for me, I wasn't in the **dark** for long.

Benjamin suggested we ask my old friend Professor Paws von Volt for help.

Professor von Volt is a brilliant scientist and inventor. We headed to his laboratory.

"Ah, yes," squeaked the professor after he had examined the photo. "There is no doubt that this is a hologram. It's a three-dimensional image that is projected and seems to be real."

He turned off the LIGHT and turned on something that looked like an old film projector. A second later, an AMAZING tropical rain forest appeared all around us!

Then we heard the most terrifying ROAR. Frozen in horror, I watched

as a ferocious TIGER materialized before us.

"G-g-g-good kitty," I squeaked, trembling with fear.

Suddenly, Benjamin and Bugsy began walking toward the beast with strange smiles on their snouts.

"NOOOOOOO!" I yelled, jumping in front of them to protect them.

But then the weirdest thing happened.

The tiger opened its jaws and . . . I passed through them without even a SCRATCH.

The professor turned on the light. "What did I tell you?" he said. "Some

holograms are so good, they seem as real as that tiger," he explained.

Benjamin hugged me. "You were very COURAGEOUS, Uncle Geronimo," he squeaked.

"Yep, we sure wouldn't want to get eaten by a hologram, Uncle G," Bugsy teased.

I coughed. Oh, how embarrassing!

Professor von Volt explained that in order to make a hologram, the projector-like machine has to be close by. Otherwise, the image will be blurred.

"So the robbers had to set up a projector somewhere near the bank," Thea reasoned.

"And I know just how they did it!" Benjamin **EXCLAIMED** suddenly.

"Me, too!" Bugsy and Thea shouted in unison.

Even Red Paparatz **chimed** in.

"Of course, it's so **OBVIOUS**!" he agreed.

"Obvious, right," I added, completely clueless. Why, oh, why was I always the last one to FIGURE things out?

Later that night, I called Benjamin and he explained everything to me.

CLUE 4

Do you know how the gang of robbers makes the cat appear?

A Large, Heavy-Duty Net

Over the next week, the Cat Gang continued to rob the banks of New Mouse City.

The **ROBBERS** followed the same routine every time. They parked their van in front of the bank.

Then they **ROBBED** the bank. When it was time to leave, they made Cat-Cat (or the hologram of Cat-Cat) chase everyone away. After that, the robbers were free to drive off with the stolen **loot**.

Even though I published an article in *The Rodent's Gazette* about the **FAKE** cat, with an interview from Professor von Volt, no one in New Mouse City believed me.

Even the mayor, **Frederick Fuzzypaws**, insisted that the **terrifying** Cat-Cat was as real as whiskers on a **mouse**. He told everyone not to worry because the police had a plan.

"The police have constructed a large, heavy-duty NET," Mayor Fuzzypaws explained. "When I give the word, they will throw the net over the giant cat and catch him!"

Of course, the plan didn't work. The giant cat walked right through the net without blinking an eye. The police went home discouraged and empty-pawed, and the robbers continued to steal from more banks.

Finally, I had to do something about the situation. My dear nephew must have been thinking the same thing, because later that day he called me.

"I have an idea," he said.

DON'T WORRY, UNCLE GERONIMO

We **all** met at my house.

Of course, this included Thea, Benjamin, Bugsy Wugsy, and Red Paparatz, who by now was part of the **TEAM**.

We sat around the table, talking. I tried my best to concentrate but my mind kept wandering. I had bought some cheesy donuts at the Stop and Squeak, and I couldn't take my eyes off them. Would it be rude to be the first to start munching? I was still drooling over the donuts when Benjamin began to squeak.

"We know the giant cat isn't real," Benjamin explained. "It's a hologram. But the thieves don't know we know their **SECRET**. So all we have to do is **SURPRISE** them!"

Suddenly, I wasn't thinking about donuts anymore.

"S-s-s-surprise them?" I stammered. Did I mention how much I hate SURPRISES?

"Don't worry, Uncle Geronimo," Benjamin replied, giving me a kiss. "We'll be okay."

I melted. How could I say no to my sweet nephew?

Subtract, Don't Add!

Benjamin took out a map.

"I marked all of the banks in the city on this map," he explained. "There are TEN altogether. So far the thieves have broken into FIVE of those banks —"

"That means there are FIFTEEN banks left!" Red Paparatz interrupted. "I'm good with math."

Bugsy ROLLED her eyes. "You need to subtract, not add," she corrected him. "There were ten banks and they already robbed five. That means there are FIVE left!"

"I knew that," Red said, turning as **red** as his hair. "Ten minus five equals **FIVE**. Any mouselet knows that one."

$$10-5=5$$

"Anyway," Benjamin continued. "There are five banks left to watch. So I drew a line from all the banks that have been robbed to all the ones left. The outline formed a **SHAPE**. Can you tell what it is?"

Rodent Savings Bank
2
Bank of New Mouse City
1
Capitol Cheese Bank
10
Pawlenders Financial
9
3
Credit Bank of Mouse Island
4
Bank of the Rat
5
Mouse Trust Bank
6
Ratfur Federal
7
Mouse Savings Bank
8
Whiskers and Loan

Benjamin's Plan

Benjamin spread the map on the table and we all stared at it.

"It's the face of a cat!" Red Paparatz shouted. "I'm good with PICTURES."

This time, he was right.

"Exactly!" Benjamin agreed. "The cat is the symbol of the gang of robbers."

"So if the thieves are going to finish the cat DESIGN, then we just have to figure out which bank they will hit next," Bugsy added.

I shivered. This plan was getting more fur-raising by the minute!

Oh, what a rodent's nightmare!

Then, just when I thought things couldn't get any SCARIER, they did.

"AUNT THEA, can you and Uncle Geronimo please follow the robbers' van with your motorcycle?" Benjamin asked sweetly.

My daredevil sister, Thea, was happy to help.

"When do we leave?" she squeaked excitedly.

I felt faint. Forget the Cat Gang! Riding on Thea's motorcycle was way more terrifying!

"I think I'm g-g-g-getting SICK," I stammered. "M-m-m-maybe I should stay behind."

But no one was listening.

"After you spot the van, Bugsy and I, along with Professor von Volt, will take action," Benjamin was saying.

Professor von Volt was coming? I started to ask Benjamin if the professor

could take my place on THEA'S motorcycle, but Thea interrupted.

"There's only one problem with your plan, Benjamin," my sister said. "You see, even if we are able to find the Cat Gang's van, and if we are able to figure out which bank they will strike next, we will have no idea when they will strike."

Benjamin grinned. "That would be true, Aunt Thea, if Bugsy hadn't checked the days and the hours of the robberies. She **discovered** they follow a pattern."

	Bank	Day	Time
Robbery #1	Bank of New Mouse City	Monday 15	3 p.m.
Robbery #2	Rodent Savings Bank	Tuesday 16	4 p.m.
Robbery #3	Credit Bank of Mouse Island	Wednesday 17	5 p.m.
Robbery #4	Bank of the Rat	Monday 22	3 p.m.
Robbery #5	Mouse Trust Bank	Tuesday 23	4 p.m.
Robbery #6	Ratfur Federal or Capitol Cheese Bank	?	?

Bugsy showed us a chart she had made of all of the robberies. It listed the names of the banks robbed and the DATE and TIME of each robbery.

I stared at the chart closely.

Holey cheese! There was a pattern!

CLUE 5

Try to complete the sequence: What day and time will robbery #6 take place?

Keep Your Eyes Open!

The next robbery would be on Wednesday the twenty-fourth at 5 P.M. And so at 4:45 P.M. on Wednesday, we put Operation Catch the Cat Gang in motion.

Benjamin, Bugsy, and Red Paparatz stayed with Professor von Volt while Thea and I got on her motorcyle.

"Ready, Gerry Berry?" my sister asked, revving the engine.

I was ready all right. Ready to JUMP off that scary motorcycle, run home, and hide under the covers! But what could I do?

"Sure," I muttered, holding on for dear life! Oh, how I hate **motorcycles**!

With a roar, the bike **ZIGZAGGED** through the streets of the city. Even though I know Thea is a skilled driver, I kept my eyes **closed** the whole time.

It took us ten minutes to complete the run between Ratfur Federal and Capitol Cheese Bank. But when we reached the place where we had started, we still hadn't spotted the van. And it was 5 p.m. exactly!

"We're going to have to do that again," Thea declared. "And this time, try keeping your eyes OPEN, Gerrykins!"

Ooops! Maybe that's why I hadn't spotted the van!

We took off again at an alarming speed. I was scared squeakless! Still, I practiced taking some deep breaths and forced myself to remain calm. It worked! Just then, I spotted the van!

Do you also see the
Cat Gang's van?

Solution: The van is parked on the street at the corner near Ratfur Federal bank.

MEEEOOOWWW!

Thea called Professor von Volt and the others to let them know we had found the van. Then we went back to the front of the bank.

I could hardly believe my eyes. The VAN was there, parked on a side street. And judging by the beam of light that came from the side facing the bank, they were already projecting the cat inside the building!

Before long, Professor von Volt arrived with Benjamin, **Red**, and Bugsy. The professor was also driving

a van, which he parked in front of the bank.

I was a nervous wreck, but the professor was relaxed.

"Let's wait until they finish the ROBBERY," he said with a chuckle.

How could the professor remain so calm? By now my fur was standing on end!

A few minutes later, the door to the bank **FLEW** open and the four robbers strode out. They were followed by the terrifying **Cat-Cat**.

Even though I knew he wasn't real, my heart began to pound like crazy.

"Remain calm!" the professor yelled to passersby. "It's only an optical illusion!"

Still, everyone near the bank took off and, I'm embarrassed to say, I hid behind Red Paparatz and his camera.

"Give up now!" Professor von Volt yelled at the robber rats. "We know that cat isn't real!"

The leader just glared at us.

"Oh yeah?" He smirked. "Is this REAL enough for you?"

Just then the cat let out a bloodcurdling meow that sent shivers down my spine.

"MEEEOOOWWW!"

Professor von Volt smiled.

"Not bad for a kitty," he commented. "But we brought a **real** cat."

All of a sudden, a **TIGER** twice the size of Cat-Cat appeared. The tiger opened its massive jaws and *ROARED*.

The Cat Gang took off with their tails between their legs. What a sight!

Even I had to laugh. Of course, I knew our tiger was fake. The first time I had met him was in Professor von Volt's lab!

The Cat Gang Is Captured!

The next day, Red Paparatz's photos were all over the front page of *The Rodent's Gazette*. **CAT GANG CAPTURED!** the headline declared. The **PAPERS** practically **flew** off the shelves.

I was so happy. The bad guys were behind bars, and I could finally relax in my cozy mousehole and enjoy the beautiful **autumn** leaves . . . or maybe the **spring** flowers . . . or the **wintry** snow-capped mountains . . .

That's right! I can enjoy all four seasons at once if I want to. How?

17 Swiss Cheese Center
New Mouse City
Geronimo Stilton, Publisher
www.geronimostilton.com
The Rodent's Gazette
CAT GANG CAPTURED!

It's easy! After we captured the **Cat Gang**, Professor von Volt gave me a gift: a digital projector and some incredible holograms!

Now I can sit on my couch and visit the most amazing places in the world! Of course, as any mouse knows, it's more fun to travel with good friends and family. And this mouse is lucky to have both!

1 Why does Thea Stilton say that it doesn't add up?
Because, according to the witness's account on page 127, there are four robbers plus the huge cat. So there should be five suspects getting into the van.

2 Look at the illustration on page 135. What does Geronimo see that is so surprising?
The Cat Gang's van is parked in front of the bank.

3 Do you notice something strange about the cat in Red Paparatz's photo on page 150?
The cat has a transparent body. You can see the bars through him. He also has no shadow.

4 Do you know how the gang of robbers makes the cat appear?
They projected it from the van.

5 Try to complete the sequence: What day and time will robbery #6 take place?
Wednesday the 24 at 5 p.m. For each robbery, the robbers add a day and an hour to the previous robbery, from Monday through Wednesday.

HOW MANY QUESTIONS DID YOU ANSWER CORRECTLY?

ALL 5 CORRECT: You are a **SUPER-SQUEAKY INVESTIGATOR!**

FROM 2 TO 4 CORRECT: You are a **SUPER INVESTIGATOR!** You'll get that added squeak soon!

LESS THAN 2 CORRECT: You are a **GOOD INVESTIGATOR!** Keep practicing to get super-squeaky!

Farewell until the next mystery!

Geronimo Stilton

GERONIMO'S JOKES

Now it's time for some fun and cheesy jokes to tickle your whiskers!

Q **Why can't a bicycle stand by itself?**

A Because it's two tired!

Q **Why did the mouse throw the clock out the window?**

A Because he wanted to see time fly!

Q **Why did the mouse need oil?**

A Because he squeaked!

Q **Why did the cat put the letter *M* into the freezer?**

A Because it turns *ice* into *mice*!

Q Why did the mouse do his homework on an airplane?

A Because he wanted a higher education!

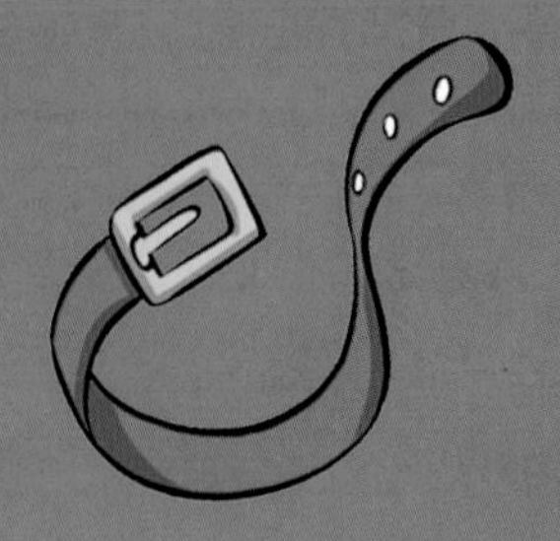

Q Why was the belt arrested?

A Because it held up some pants!

Q What kind of shoes do spies wear?

A Sneakers!

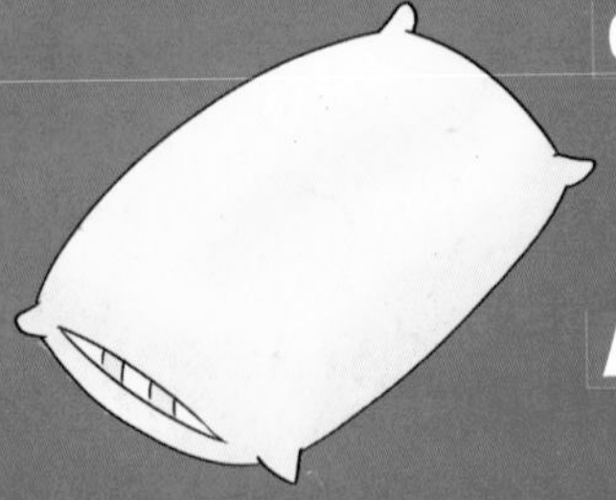

Q Why did the mouse put sugar on his pillow?

A So he could have sweet dreams!

Q **What did the duck say to the waiter?**

A "Put it on my bill!"

Q **What is a basketball player's favorite type of cheese?**

A *Swish* cheese!

Q **Why did the mouse's computer sneeze?**

A Because it had a virus!

Q **Why did the calendar feel popular?**

A Because it had a lot of dates!

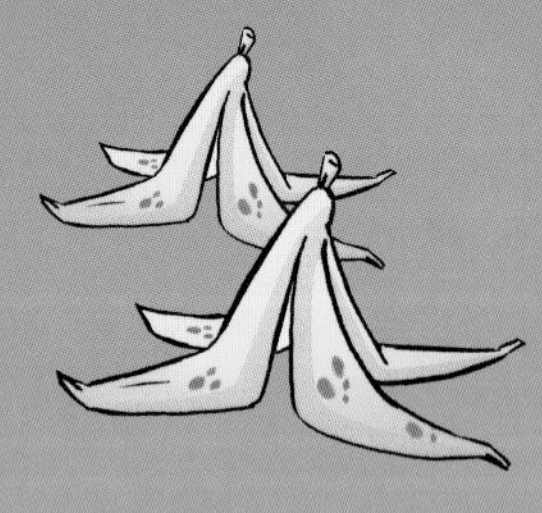

Q **What do you call two banana peels?**

A A pair of slippers!

Q **What's a cat's favorite dessert?**

A *Mice* cream!

Q **Why do fish always know their weight?**

A Because they have their own scales!

Q **How does a mouse know the ocean is friendly?**

A Because it's always *wave*-ing!

Be sure to read all my fabumouse adventures!

#1 Lost Treasure of the Emerald Eye

#2 The Curse of the Cheese Pyramid

#3 Cat and Mouse in a Haunted House

#4 I'm Too Fond of My Fur!

#5 Four Mice Deep in the Jungle

#6 Paws Off, Cheddarface!

#7 Red Pizzas for a Blue Count

#8 Attack of the Bandit Cats

#9 A Fabumouse Vacation for Geronimo

#10 All Because of a Cup of Coffee

#11 It's Halloween, You 'Fraidy Mouse!

#12 Merry Christmas, Geronimo!

#13 The Phantom of the Subway

#14 The Temple of the Ruby of Fire

#15 The Mona Mousa Code

#16 A Cheese-Colored Camper

#17 Watch Your Whiskers, Stilton!

#18 Shipwreck on the Pirate Islands

#19 My Name Is Stilton, Geronimo Stilton

#20 Surf's Up, Geronimo!

#21 The Wild, Wild West

#22 The Secret of Cacklefur Castle

A Christmas Tale

#23 Valentine's Day Disaster

#24 Field Trip to Niagara Falls

#25 The Search for Sunken Treasure

#26 The Mummy with No Name

#27 The Christmas Toy Factory

#28 Wedding Crasher

#29 Down and Out Down Under

#30 The Mouse Island Marathon

#31 The Mysterious Cheese Thief

Christmas Catastrophe

#32 Valley of the Giant Skeletons

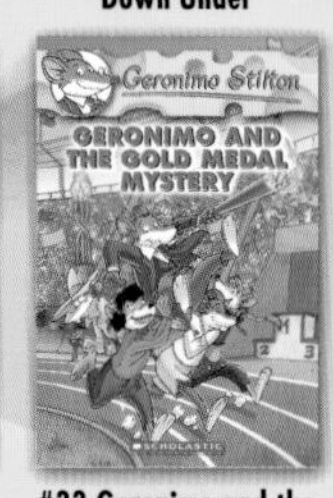

#33 Geronimo and the Gold Medal Mystery

#34 Geronimo Stilton, Secret Agent

#35 A Very Merry Christmas

#36 Geronimo's Valentine

#37 The Race Across America

#38 A Fabumouse School Adventure

#39 Singing Sensation

#40 The Karate Mouse

#41 Mighty Mount Kilimanjaro

#42 The Peculiar Pumpkin Thief

#43 I'm Not a Supermouse!

#44 The Giant Diamond Robbery

#45 Save the White Whale!

#46 The Haunted Castle

#47 Run for the Hills, Geronimo!

#48 The Mystery in Venice

#49 The Way of the Samurai

#50 This Hotel Is Haunted!

#51 The Enormouse Pearl Heist

#52 Mouse in Space!

#53 Rumble in the Jungle

#54 Get into Gear, Stilton!

#55 The Golden Statue Plot

#56 Flight of the Red Bandit

The Hunt for the Golden Book

#57 The Stinky Cheese Vacation

#58 The Super Chef Contest

#59 Welcome to Moldy Manor

The Hunt for the Curious Cheese

#60 The Treasure of Easter Island

#61 Mouse House Hunter

#62 Mouse Overboard!

The Hunt for the Secret Papyrus

#63 The Cheese Experiment

Join me and my friends as we travel through time in these very special editions!

THE JOURNEY THROUGH TIME

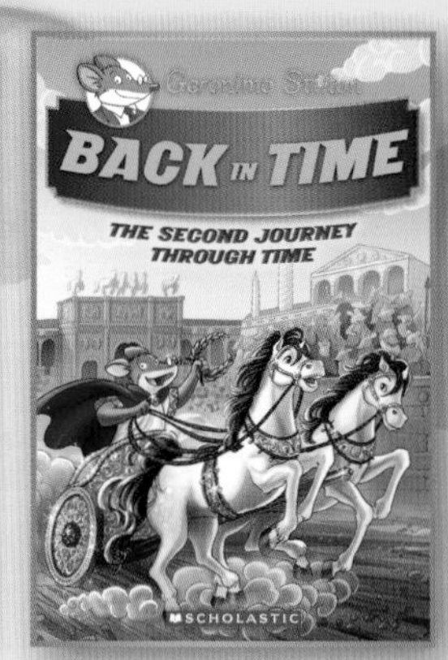

BACK IN TIME:
THE SECOND JOURNEY THROUGH TIME

THE RACE AGAINST TIME:
THE THIRD JOURNEY THROUGH TIME

MEET
Geronimo Stiltonord

He is a mouseking — the Geronimo Stilton of the ancient far north! He lives with his brawny and brave clan in the village of Mouseborg. From sailing frozen waters to facing fiery dragons, *every* day is an adventure for the micekings!

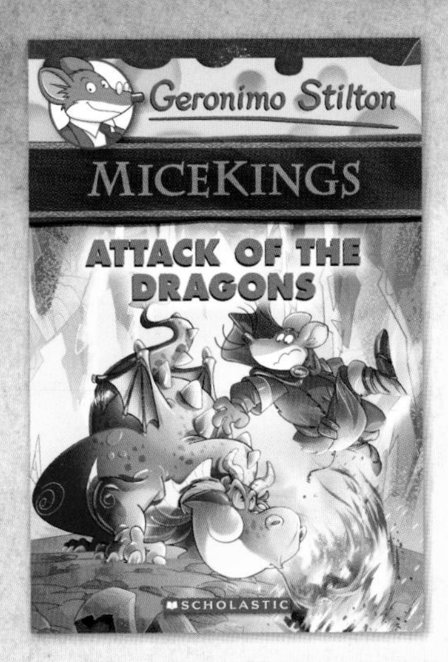

#1 Attack of the Dragons

#2 The Famouse Fjord Race

THE KINGDOM OF FANTASY

THE QUEST FOR PARADISE:
THE RETURN TO THE KINGDOM OF FANTASY

THE AMAZING VOYAGE:
THE THIRD ADVENTURE IN THE KINGDOM OF FANTASY

THE DRAGON PROPHECY:
THE FOURTH ADVENTURE IN THE KINGDOM OF FANTASY

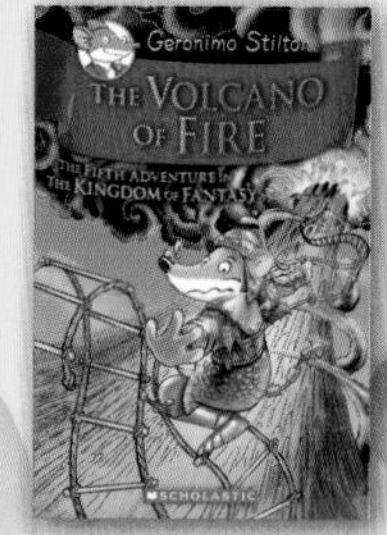

THE VOLCANO OF FIRE:
THE FIFTH ADVENTURE IN THE KINGDOM OF FANTASY

THE SEARCH FOR TREASURE:
THE SIXTH ADVENTURE IN THE KINGDOM OF FANTASY

THE ENCHANTED CHARMS:
THE SEVENTH ADVENTURE IN THE KINGDOM OF FANTASY

THE PHOENIX OF DESTINY:
AN EPIC KINGDOM OF FANTASY ADVENTURE

THE HOUR OF MAGIC:
THE EIGHTH ADVENTURE IN THE KINGDOM OF FANTASY

Don't miss any of these exciting Thea Sisters adventures!

Thea Stilton and the Dragon's Code

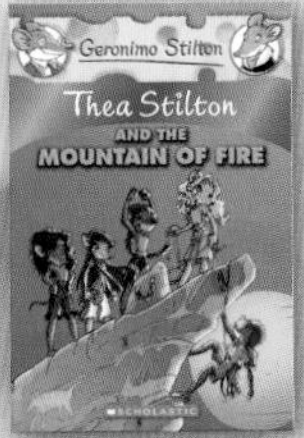

Thea Stilton and the Mountain of Fire

Thea Stilton and the Ghost of the Shipwreck

Thea Stilton and the Secret City

Thea Stilton and the Mystery in Paris

Thea Stilton and the Cherry Blossom Adventure

Thea Stilton and the Star Castaways

Thea Stilton: Big Trouble in the Big Apple

Thea Stilton and the Ice Treasure

Thea Stilton and the Secret of the Old Castle

Thea Stilton and the Blue Scarab Hunt

Thea Stilton and the Prince's Emerald

Thea Stilton and the Mystery on the Orient Express

Thea Stilton and the Dancing Shadows

Thea Stilton and the Legend of the Fire Flowers

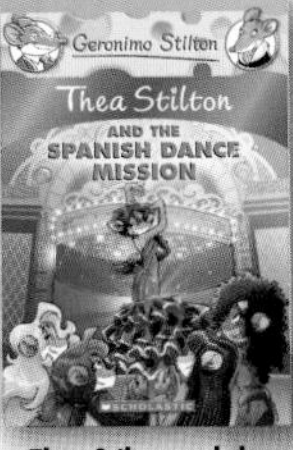

Thea Stilton and the Spanish Dance Mission

Thea Stilton and the Journey to the Lion's Den

Thea Stilton and the Great Tulip Heist

Thea Stilton and the Chocolate Sabotage

Thea Stilton and the Missing Myth

Thea Stilton and the Lost Letters

Thea Stilton and the Tropical Treasure

Thea Stilton and the Hollywood Hoax

MEET GERONIMO STILTONIX

He is a spacemouse — the Geronimo Stilton of a parallel universe! He is captain of the spaceship *MouseStar 1*. While flying through the cosmos, he visits distant planets and meets crazy aliens. His adventures are out of this world!

#1 Alien Escape

#2 You're Mine, Captain!

#3 Ice Planet Adventure

#4 The Galactic Goal

#5 Rescue Rebellion

#6 The Underwater Planet

#7 Beware! Space Junk!

Meet GERONIMO STILTONOOT

He is a cavemouse — Geronimo Stilton's ancient ancestor! He runs the stone newspaper in the prehistoric village of Old Mouse City. From dealing with dinosaurs to dodging meteorites, his life in the Stone Age is full of adventure!

#1 The Stone of Fire

#2 Watch Your Tail!

#3 Help, I'm in Hot Lava!

#4 The Fast and the Frozen

#5 The Great Mouse Race

#6 Don't Wake the Dinosaur!

#7 I'm a Scaredy-Mouse!

#8 Surfing for Secrets

#9 Get the Scoop, Geronimo!

#10 My Autosaurus Will Win!

#11 Sea Monster Surprise

ABOUT THE AUTHOR

Born in New Mouse City, Mouse Island, **GERONIMO STILTON** is Rattus Emeritus of Mousomorphic Literature and of Neo-Ratonic Comparative Philosophy. For the past twenty years, he has been running *The Rodent's Gazette*, New Mouse City's most widely read daily newspaper.

Stilton was awarded the Ratitzer Prize for his scoops on *The Curse of the Cheese Pyramid* and *The Search for Sunken Treasure.* He has also received the Andersen 2000 Prize for Personality of the Year. One of his bestsellers won the 2002 eBook Award for world's best ratlings' electronic book. His works have been published all over the globe.

In his spare time, Mr. Stilton collects antique cheese rinds and plays golf. But what he most enjoys is telling stories to his nephew Benjamin.

6
5
4
3
2
1
1. Main entrance
2. Printing presses (where the books and newspaper are printed)
3. Accounts department
4. Editorial room (where the editors, illustrators, and designers work)
5. Geronimo Stilton's office
6. Helicopter landing pad
THE RODENT'S GAZETTE

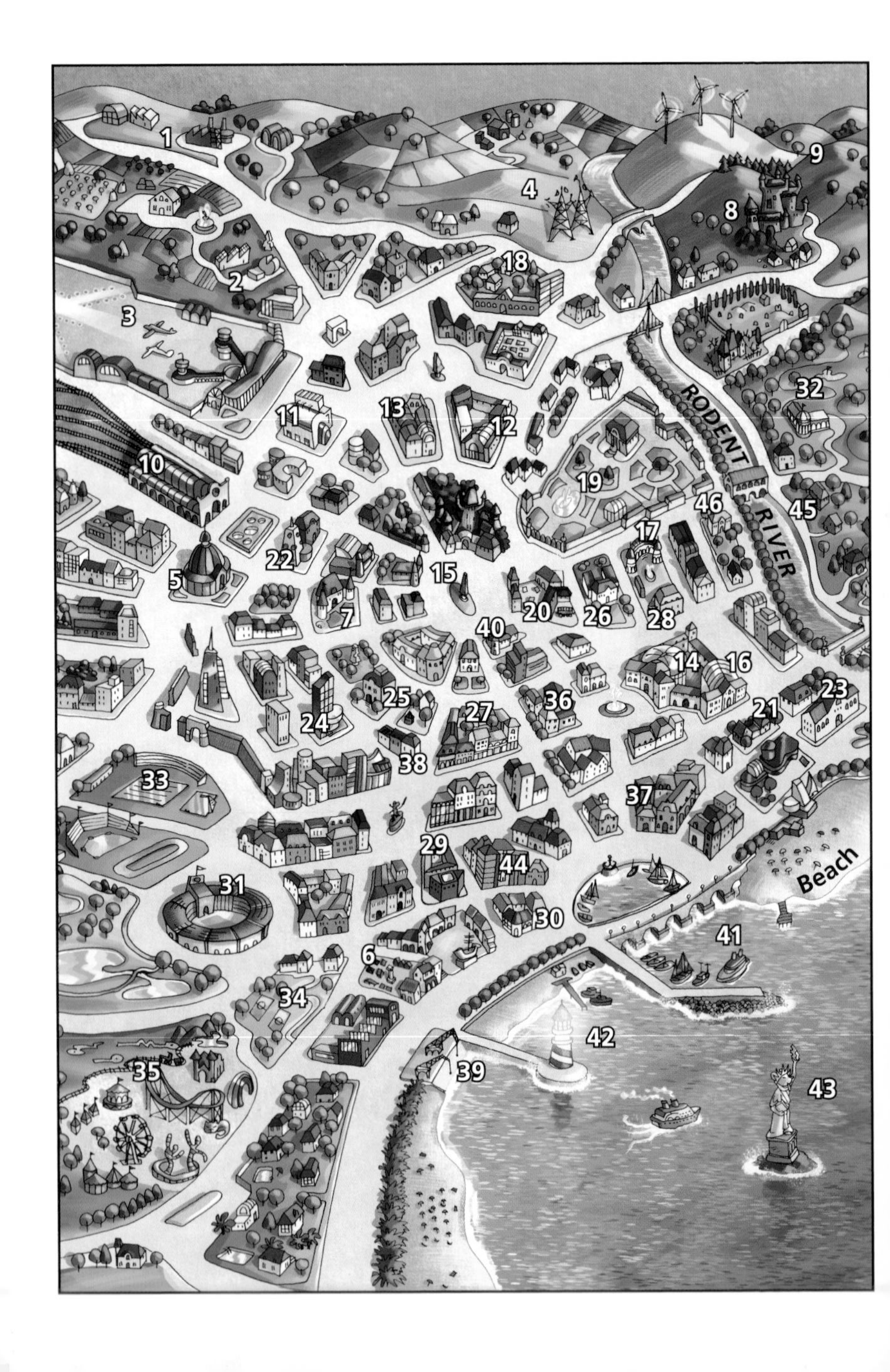

1
2
3
4
5
6
7
8
9
10
11
12
13
14
15
16
17
18
19
20
21
22
23
24
25
26
27
28
29
30
31
32
33
34
35
36
37
38
39
40
41
42
43
44
45
46
RODENT
RIVER
Beach

Map of New Mouse City

1. Industrial Zone
2. Cheese Factories
3. Angorat International Airport
4. WRAT Radio and Television Station
5. Cheese Market
6. Fish Market
7. Town Hall
8. Snotnose Castle
9. The Seven Hills of Mouse Island
10. Mouse Central Station
11. Trade Center
12. Movie Theater
13. Gym
14. Catnegie Hall
15. Singing Stone Plaza
16. The Gouda Theater
17. Grand Hotel
18. Mouse General Hospital
19. Botanical Gardens
20. Cheap Junk for Less (Trap's store)
21. Aunt Sweetfur and Benjamin's House
22. Mouseum of Modern Art
23. University and Library
24. *The Daily Rat*
25. *The Rodent's Gazette*
26. Trap's House
27. Fashion District
28. The Mouse House Restaurant
29. Environmental Protection Center
30. Harbor Office
31. Mousidon Square Garden
32. Golf Course
33. Swimming Pool
34. Tennis Courts
35. Curlyfur Island Amousement Park
36. Geronimo's House
37. Historic District
38. Public Library
39. Shipyard
40. Thea's House
41. New Mouse Harbor
42. Luna Lighthouse
43. The Statue of Liberty
44. Hercule Poirat's Office
45. Petunia Pretty Paws's House
46. Grandfather William's House

This way to the Rodent Straits
Brigand's Isle
Tomcat Island
Pirate Ship of Cats
Hamster Islands
Blue Dolphin Bay
Coral Reefs
This way to the Mousific Ocean
Stray Cat Harbor
San Mouscisco
Cat's Claw Bay
Panther Archipelago
Swissville
Cheddarton
Mouseport
This way to the Ratlantic Ocean
New Mouse City
Mousefort Beach
Furflung Island
This way to the Sea of Mice
N
W
E
S
MOUSE ISLAND
1
2
3
4
5
6
7
8
9
10
11
12
13
14
15
16
17
18
19
20
21
22
23
24
25
26
27
28
29
30
31
32
33
34
35
36
37

Map of Mouse Island

1. Big Ice Lake
2. Frozen Fur Peak
3. Slipperyslopes Glacier
4. Coldcreeps Peak
5. Ratzikistan
6. Transratania
7. Mount Vamp
8. Roastedrat Volcano
9. Brimstone Lake
10. Poopedcat Pass
11. Stinko Peak
12. Dark Forest
13. Vain Vampires Valley
14. Goose Bumps Gorge
15. The Shadow Line Pass
16. Penny Pincher Castle
17. Nature Reserve Park
18. Las Ratayas Marinas
19. Fossil Forest
20. Lake Lake
21. Lake Lakelake
22. Lake Lakelakelake
23. Cheddar Crag
24. Cannycat Castle
25. Valley of the Giant Sequoia
26. Cheddar Springs
27. Sulfurous Swamp
28. Old Reliable Geyser
29. Vole Vale
30. Ravingrat Ravine
31. Gnat Marshes
32. Munster Highlands
33. Mousehara Desert
34. Oasis of the Sweaty Camel
35. Cabbagehead Hill
36. Rattytrap Jungle
37. Rio Mosquito

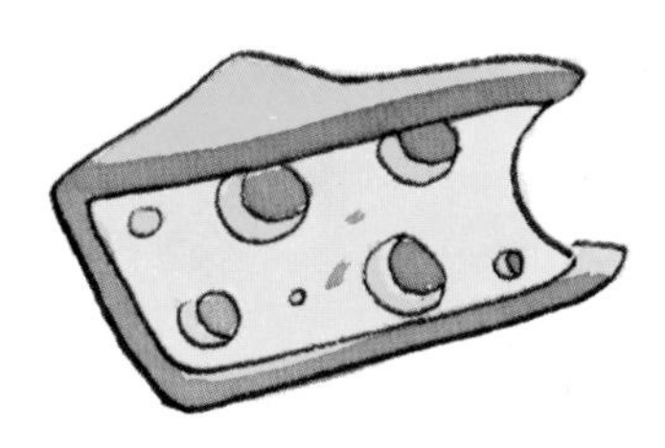

Dear mouse friends,
Thanks for reading, and farewell
till the next book.
It'll be another whisker-licking-good
adventure, and that's a promise!

Geronimo Stilton